The End of the Legend of Jared Snead

Theron Montgomery

Boat Shop Press

Boat Shop Press, November 2016

Copyright © Theron Montgomery, 2009

Published in the United States by Boat Shop Press

Cover art designed by Eric Wayne Key. Photography by Greg Warren
Published in the United States by Boat Shop Press
Boat Shop Press **ISBN**: 978-0692837795
www.boatshoppress.com
Printed in the United States of America
10 9 8 7 6 5 4 3 2 1

To the memory of Cathi Word Downing

"The end occurs not at the end..."   "The End" by Nadia Herman Colburn

In early fall of 1971, I was stationed with a Ranger combat platoon in Bien Hoa, Vietnam, applying for a third tour, ever intent on avenging the death of Foster Odom, my lifelong and best friend from Fermata Bend, Alabama, who had been killed a year before by a Viet Cong sniper. And it was at that same time I received a brief letter from my mother informing me that Jared Snead, Foster's great uncle, was dead. Mother mailed her letter with Jared Snead's front page obituary clipping from the *Fermata Bend Bugler*, just as she had mailed me the one on Foster a year ago, and the ones before that on the likes of Todd Newman and Curtis Johnson, who were Killed In Action, too, as well as the one on Bubba Smith who was listed MIA. Like the others, she underlined in blue ink particular columned paragraphs for me to take note of. *Beck*, she wrote at the end of her letter, *when it was all over, I asked your father if this was the end of an era. He wouldn't answer, he just looked off.*

I remembered how she wrote, *All Fermata Bend Mourns* on the edge of Foster's obituary clipping. And like Foster's, the top of Jared Snead's obituary carried a large, up-close, black and white photograph of a young, clear-eyed man smiling at you from another time, in a stiff collar and a tie. In his youth, Jared Snead had looked something like Foster, only with wider cheeks and a milder, calmer look in the eye. I got the sense, the feeling, they were similar youths from Fermata Bend, clear-eyed and willing. *Jared Edward Snead*, the front page obituary read, *one of Fermata Bend's most distinguished family sons and veterans, was found dead Wednesday in the woods adjacent his family home place. He was eighty-two.*

Jared Snead, or "The Teller of the Tales," as our small town fondly referred to him, was found frozen to death against the trunk of a massive old oak in the woods beyond the overgrown field by his home place. We boys had grown up taught by the men to respect him. We imitated his social manners. We ate his camp stew and sweet potatoes with the veterans in the dusty parlor of his old home place after Escatawpha Hunting Club deer drives, standing around in our hunting clothes and boots on the bare, worn floorboards, among dark and stoic family portraits on the sallow walls, holding old, chipped china bowls and tarnished silver dinner spoons in our hands, balancing paper napkins and tall, paper Dixie Cups of sweet tea. There was a dull brass Pier mirror, a stuffed duchesse and a small, dark, boxy-looking piano that General Beauregard had once played in the dining room. Jared Snead played it for us again, seating himself, baring his gray head and wizened face, the yellowed piano keys plinking under his gnarled fingers as we boys stood around with the men and sang with him, "Lorena" or "The Yellow Rose of Texas."

I grew up in Fermata Bend, Alabama, believing in Jared Snead and the veterans. I grew up listening to Jared Snead punctuate his talk with long, low whistles as though to sound an exclamation. I grew up listening to and watching my father's weathered face grin among the men. I heard him and them talk of hunting, crops, politics, sports or war, standing around with the men at the hardware, the Co-Op, the post office or the barber shop. In front of those men, my father told a joke, laughed, put his arm around my neck and knuckled my hair; he slipped me sticks of Beemans; he bragged to the men about the buck I bagged or the double play I made at the baseball game. The veterans of Fermata Bend ran the hunts, they coached Little League, and they headed the Boy Scouts troop. And like Jared Snead, my father and the veterans imparted a belief with their constant talk on us boys that being an American and a Southerner was a great thing; being an American was somehow Right and a patriotic duty; and being a soldier, however terrible, was a courageous act and a rite to manhood.

Jared Snead's aged and wizened face would spread out his long, gray and unkempt beard whenever he smiled, revealing old and stained teeth; he had proud, dark and curious eyes; a shrill cackle and a booming guffaw; he chewed tobacco and used the old words, like *rife, lief* and *yonder*. He wore old, hand-me-down clothes and drove a wagon and mule or would peddle a rusty bicycle, doing odd jobs and selling firewood, sweet potatoes or pecans around the town square. At church, he would kneel in the old family pew and make the loudest "Amens" at the end of prayers. He nodded and spoke to every white man and most blacks; he swept off his battered, brown fedora, smiled and bowed his head slightly for every woman, stepping off the front porch and into the yard if the woman came to the front door and the man of the house was not present.

Jared Snead, "The Teller of the Tales," was the oldest of the veterans and of the Pecan Families in Fermata Bend. He was the oldest herald of history in our community, and often, in some way, a part of everything, of everyone, in the middle of the world of us white men and boys. We knew, saw and heard him in his worn hunting coat, his coarse gray beard and his battered brown fedora while he told the war stories and the town tales around the campfires when the Escatawpha Hunting Club ran the hounds for foxes and raccoons, or at the Co-Op, the hardware, the post office and the barber shop in town. And we listened. When he told the stories, his dark, aged eyes widened, his voice quivered between his whistles with a shrill vitality and a belief that history was significant, a permanent record; the proof of truth virtually in the telling, itself: tales of Hernando De Soto and Chief Tuscaloosa, Andrew Jackson and the Red Sticks; Bedford Forrest, Joe Wheeler and General Beauregard's campaigns in Alabama and particularly Escatawpha County. He told of his father's war in Cuba, The Great War that he had been in, when the "Dixie" Division broke the Hindenburg Line. He would stop and let our fathers and the other veterans tell us of what they knew, too, of, say, Wilson's Raiders in Alabama during the Civil War, War World Two and Korea: D-Day, The Battle of the Bulge, Iwo Jima, then the Yalu River or Operation Ripper.

What Jared Snead's obituary did not tell was how in his poverty, ever since the Great Depression, the families of Fermata Bend accommodated him. The man who never owned a TV or air conditioning had people to listen to him. He had food, hand-me-downs and odd jobs because he had family history and was looked up to as a model from the past. Every fall, the veterans let Jared Snead lead the Veterans' Day Parade down Main Street and around the square in an overcoat and

Dough Boy helmet, beating the march time on an old bass drum. He bathed and wore his grandfather's frayed tuxedo to the Veterans' Ball, where he made the emcee's speech, praising the greatness of Escatawpha county soldiers who had served for generations, many whose faces stared down on us from still photos and daguerreotypes on the wood-planked armory walls. After Jared Snead's speech, he danced with each of the ladies in their formals, too, over the old heart-pine floorboards, and took down the old sword General Beauregard had presented to the town from the mantle of the rock fireplace for us boys to hold and pass. Among the photographs on the wall of the town armory were two, faded and framed, black and white photographs of Jared Snead, one of him young and grim-faced in a World War One uniform; the other of him still young and smiling in a suit and a touring cap for the camera, posed in a still shot and carrying his new bride in a long, draped wedding gown over the threshold into the family home place, a Pecan Family tradition. She is young, thin, and smiling at the camera, too, before she died childless in 1929. The caption below reads: *Carrying her towards another Fermata Bend family and home.*

The last time, Mom wrote in her accompanying letter, *you knew who to write to, that being Lisa Nanner,* she wrote, meaning Foster's mother. *But now, there's no one,* she added. *Where does it go?* Her letter went on to relate how the older citizens of Fermata Bend turned out to march in Jared Snead's funeral procession, quietly milling and following the veterans marching in their Sunday suits and blue veterans caps, behind the U.S. flag-draped casket on a wagon, drawn by a horse and led by one of the veterans in an old Dough Boy uniform. The funeral march went around the town square and out and down the county highway where the town veterans eventually buried Jared Snead in the winter pasture of his old family home place, along with a prayer, a speech and a twenty-one gun salute, vowing to hold a vigil for him each year.

When it was all over, I asked your father if this was the end of an era, my mom wrote at the end of her letter. *He wouldn't answer, he just looked off.*

The morning after my follow-up request for a third tour was denied, I woke up in my briefs and dog tags, alone with a parched mouth and a pounding head in Vin Trough's small futon bed above the Paradise Bar. I crawled down the narrow, tiled hallway of stale vomit and burnt hash under the slow rattan fans, threw up in the pull-chain toilet, gulped bottled water and passed out on the floor. Later, I came to in a thick sweat and my head in a slow spin. I rose and staggered back into Vin Trough's room and dressed in my fatigues before her gilded dressing mirror, smoking the last pinch of her dope on the small, teak table and dropping what piasters I had left to the floor. Making my way down the hallway, down the spiral bamboo stairway and through the bead string blinds into the thick, stale air of last night's cigarette smoke, hashish and beer, I crossed the dim and vacant concrete barroom of jumbled cocktail tables and chairs toward the front doors.

Vin Trough's sudden and sharp cry cut through the stillness but I didn't stop. I heard something of her voice again, heard panting, the quick tapping of high heels. At the front double wooden doors, I turned with a ready, steeled smile to face her coming toward me, her wide, frightened eyes and parting mouth of red lips and bleached teeth; the stark fear of her look that I would desert her, too, as everyone else had; I would leave, too, with no hope for anything else. Her heavy eyelashes and shiny blush, her silky black bangs and bright yellow bar dress, made her seem in the early morning like an over-dressed, ridiculous doll. *Clown*, I thought of her with a sneer. Vin Trough stared. Her mouth moved. She stopped hard, slipped and fell, her mouth open in both her fear and astonishment as she went back and down, her sheer-hosed legs and high heels sprawling over the littered, concrete floor; her fine black hair splaying over the heavy, made-up face. I looked at her and I didn't help her up.

"*Tai Sao?*" she cried at me, sitting up. "*Tai Sao?*"

"You're just temporary," I said, grinning mean. I looked at her and thought how I could kill her with my hands if I wanted to, and then something of Marica came to me, my old girl friend back home, whom I could never kill, but whom I knew I had lost forever, in my rage and grief; in following my sense of loyalty and memory of Foster Odom, in being worthy of him and the men and friends I had known all my life in Fermata Bend. Signing up for the second tour was all I could think to do, what the veterans back home would have respected me for doing.

I turned away from Vin Trough while she stared up at me from the floor and I felt at that moment that what I had just said to her was true for everything I had done since coming to Vietnam. Everything was futile. "*Cam On,*" I said, hitting the double doors open on my palms and never looking back again, going out into the sudden, blinding glare and blanket of humidity and sunlight, into the throngs of small, dark-haired people in thin and bland clothing, rubber sandals, bare-headed or in conical hats, chattering animatedly in Vietnamese; the littered, smoky back streets lined with vendors and their make-shift wooden, cardboard or bamboo stands; the smell of fresh and rotting fruit, incense, dog meat and patchouli oil; the sporadic, noisy passing of rickshaws and motor scooters. Mother had written, in one of her ever-regular and dutiful letters, that Marica had become engaged to a soybean farmer somewhere south of Citronelle.

I stumbled down the back streets of Bien Hoa, through Vietnamese people, determined to find my platoon and get drunk with them before they were ordered out and my Freedom Bird was scheduled to leave, feeling the disconnect since coming to Vietnam, between what I had come from, what I had been brought up to be, and what I had become, knowing for a year now that there was no true revenge for Foster Odom's death, no revenge for my rage at losing him and losing something of myself in him, and now with no good faith or reason for breaking my promise to Marica Brown, except a fierce, hard pride imparted on me by the veterans of my and Foster's childhood of being able to return home and look everyone, especially all the men, in the face.

The Disconnect.

Damn you, Beck Senecal. Marica wrote me in her arched handwriting of watery, sky blue ink on her ever clean, peach parchment with small bird vignettes in the corners, after I had written her a year ago that I would not be coming home as I had promised, but would be signing on for a second tour to avenge the death of Foster Odom. *Damn you boys of Fermata Bend,* she wrote. *Damn your lot, your honor and your notion of manhood. I am not Pecan Family, my father's not from here,* she went on, *and I am the pharmacist's daughter, remember?* She berated the ways and bonding of Fermata Bend men.

She called me names, telling me how I had broken her heart and how single-minded, stupid and cruel the entire Fermata Bend male species was. *And so, well, here's hoping you don't die, Beck Senecal,* she closed, *but if you do, it'll be your own fault. I stopped praying for you two days ago and I won't be sitting home alone anymore on Saturday nights. I'll not be second to anyone. Put that in your gun and shoot it.*

    I had read her letter in disbelief. I had assumed she would understand. I had thought she knew what it meant to be a boy or a man from Fermata Bend and to be able to come home and look everyone in the face again who had known and loved Foster Odom, my best friend, and the best of us who had volunteered Delayed Entry out of our high school class in typical Pecan Family tradition. I imagined her reading her letter out loud to me, teary-eyed, hard-toned and sarcastic. Marica Brown, the town's pharmacist's daughter, with her long, deep-red hair; the slightly lifted corner of her mouth, in a small and wry slant when she smiled; who wore jeans and t-shirts and chewed Dentyne red gum whenever she could and who would cock one knee at rest whenever she stood still for long, as a horse will do with a back leg when standing still. Her steady, staid gaze of gray eyes would make me swallow and I saw and heard her sing "My Green Tambourine" with the wind in her hair as we rode horseback. She was quiet, a tomboy and a loner. I was in love with her presence, her gaze, and her no nonsense. She didn't wear makeup. She preferred to be with dogs and horses. She didn't talk about herself and she didn't seek the company of the prim and proper, Fermata Bend family girls.

    Now never mind you that, Mother wrote to me after Marica's final letter, on her own short, plain alabaster parchment with her small and even lines of short, cursive letters in a deeper blue ink. *She's a sweet girl, but you need someone who knows the ways and will be steadfast, like real Pecan Family. Her daddy is a good man--but, you know--he's an outsider and her mother is only a cousin of the Wellborns.*

In the bottom of Marica's last peach-colored envelope to me, I found the silver chain with the brooch locket containing a lock of my hair which I had given her on the night of our high school graduation, the old, traditional gift of soldiers to their sweethearts in Fermata Bend. In the bottom of the envelope, also, I found the Coke tab ring I had pulled off my canned drink on our last and warm fall night together, seated on the swing of her parents' back porch during my leave before shipping out, with the still, heavy odor of begonias, fresh-mowed grass and a steady, pulsating hum of a tree frog in the distance while we sat in a long, awkward pause of finality, me not knowing what else to say before I said goodbye. I took her hand and slid the tab ring onto her little finger and mumbled, *"Wait for me,"* recalling Fermata Bend courting stories of soldiers in the Civil War, how my grandfather had asked my grandmother to wait for him in World War One and my father had asked my mother to wait for him in World War Two.

Marica surprised me by staring at me, looking away, suddenly stifling a sob and covering her face in her hands. "You are going to carry me across the threshold?" she said, in a tone of disbelief. "You want me to cook your meals and darn your socks? Make a family in Fermata Bend?" To which I said, "Yes" and nodded, because I couldn't think of doing anything else nor of anyone else I wanted to do it with; and she nodded and smiled, too, so hopeful, so fast and emphatic that for a moment I thought she was having a spasm of apoplexy.

It was the only time I saw her cry, though she had taken the
news of my signing up Delayed Entry with Foster Odom and
other Fermata Bend boys with a look of blanched horror and
disbelief, glaring me in, glassy-eyed from the front passenger's
seat of my SS Camaro on that cool spring night, when I told
her on the town square, parked at the curb before her father's
drug store while we ate orange push-up Pixies and listened
to Bobby Goldsboro's "Little Green Apples" as it came softly
over the car radio. I told her after she informed me she was
going to go to our Escatawpha Junior College. Her stare froze
rigid on me throughout the song and into a Phisohex liquid
soap commercial and even into the soft tune of a Benson and
Hedges 100s commercial--the cigarette that lasts a "long, long
time," while her lips glistened liquid orange under the light
from the drug store windows.

"So you're going." She made it a terse statement, her
look flushed and pained, as though it had become hard for
her to breathe or as though she had just been struck in the
face. "You're going like the rest of them?" she stared. "It's you
men," she said. "It's always you men."

I didn't know what to say to that, but she knew perfectly
well the answer, because she was from Fermata Bend, too,
and boys from Fermata Bend grew up impressed upon by the
other boys and men to be like them, to be accepted as hunt-
ers, athletes and soldiers. It struck me as odd that she would
consider me to be different.

"I can't not," I finally said. "Fighting for your country
is the right thing to do," I echoed the boys. I echoed Jared
Snead. I echoed the veterans. I echoed war comics and Saturday night TV.

She stared at me with her still, gray eyes and a speechless
and baffled expression, as though she was cursed and privi-
leged to some wisdom let to her and denied to me.

"It's the men," Marica said with a long, slow pause. "Y'all see yourselves in each other. Y'all see yourselves."

She held her eyes on me. I couldn't say anything to that, either. I hadn't thought that far, only of what was coming first, what I felt was expected of me to do, like going out for football or baseball in order to be one of the boys and because it was expected from the men and because there was little else to do in Fermata Bend; only this was bigger, thinking, somehow, in the back of my mind, the rest would somehow work out later, it would fall into place.

But the morning after I mumbled, *Wait for me,* and slid my Coke tab ring onto her finger, she resigned herself and took it for what it was, as a gesture of commitment, and made a point to go with me and my parents and see me off at the train station in Mobile. We sat together in the back seat of my parents' maroon Oldsmobile 88, holding hands. I was in my khaki uniform. I can't remember if she was in a blue or a yellow Sunday dress. I can't remember if it was a sunny, cloudy or rainy day. What I remember is a numbness at the edge of everything, a feeling of going through forced and calm motions; my parents in their Sunday clothes in the front seat and then standing off on the concrete platform at the train station with brave and smiling faces after hugging me goodbye; Marica swallowing and coming up to me, as though accepting a duty; her rich, red hair; her soft, humid smell of Dove soap and Wind Song perfume. She swallowed, hugged and kissed me hard in front of my parents on the concrete platform and uttered something like a fierce whisper into my mouth before we parted. I didn't know what she said, but the volume of it vibrated in my teeth with her hard, bland breath and it felt, I realized later, like a plea for strength.

"I'll be waiting for you here when you come back," she whispered, after we parted. *"One year from now,"* she held up her index finger. *"Promise."* I nodded. *"Promise,"* I said. Her intent gray eyes peered up at me and her mouth curled into that small, wry slant. *"You come back now,"* she said. *"You will come back."* And then she made a smile for me. Only, it did not hide her fear.

In San Francisco, I walked the streets in my creased khakis and Army boots, my travel bag slung over my shoulder. I stared bewildered at the loud clothing, variety and pageantry of streaming, mostly smiling, multi-cultured Americans in the mild air, under a clear and infinite sky. Everything and everyone seemed to vibrate with motion, seemed imbued in the butter-gold light. Windshields glowed, buildings gleamed. The city was dry, vast, noisy and surreal since my Freedom Bird had landed from Bien Hoa that morning. I had eaten my last meal at the commissary and had been discharged at the Oakland Army Depot. Rather than wait for the bus, I had followed my immediate impulse, marched out the gates and begun my walk, alone and lost on the streets and the sidewalks of an American city, feeling lethargic and numb with jet lag, and as though I had been jerked out of one time into another.

My pace was slow and irregular. Eyes lingered on me, cast off and passed. About me were many different types of people, as many Asians, Hispanics and blacks as anyone else. The pace was quick. I couldn't find a rhythm. I couldn't relax, wouldn't let people come near me, making sure not to step on the cracks along the steep streets criss-crossed in trolley tracks; on the sidewalks along the colorful, glassed shops; or even on the narrow, rocked paths to the small, interspersed parks, thick with shrubs, clean flower beds and grass; and benches under swaying limbs of Eucalyptus trees.

Some blurred and numbed time later, I lowered my travel bag onto a transit bench at an intersection and lit a cigarette on my steel Zippo, stood and smoked and stared in the traffic, taking in the noise, the confusion, the tempo; the different races, clothes and hairstyles. I was back in the United States, in a city, but I felt the disconnect. The Disconnect. I heard the slow *plinking* of General Beauregard's piano on the floorboards of Jared Snead's decadent living room. I felt the presence of the men back home, saw Jared Snead's old face of belief, saw him in his battered fedora and his grin of old teeth, leading the Veterans' Parade with his drum. *"You might wonder,"* I could hear Jared Snead's shrill voice from back home; could see the old man sitting on a fence in his boots and hunting coat, squinting, grinning at me and cocking his head with his coarse, unkempt beard under the brown fedora. I could see him making a long, slow whistle and shaking his head in bewilderment, maybe even bemusement, at this scene. San Francisco was another place.

When I thought of my hometown, I saw dogs for some reason, quiet streets, framed, wooden houses and old trees; remembered the dull lethargy of lazy, hot summers; the slow town square, the smell of dirt roads and the river. But most of all, I remembered the men, saw them fanning out of the woods like troopers in their hunting boots and coats; their taunts, jeers and laughs; the ones who talked, the ones we boys heard all of our lives, and led by the likes of Jared Snead.

They were mostly town merchants and farmers, almost all of them veterans, many of them continuing in the National Guard--their groupings and actions and talk all inclusive, their world the one we boys imitated.

I saw my mother and father's calm, expectant faces: crows feet at their eyes; my mother's short, steel hair and her small, worried mouth; my father's smiling, weathered face with laughing wrinkles, his thinning, brown hair; but their look infallibly calm and with a certitude that the world they lived in was definite and sure. I remembered the sense of belonging to them, a community and a church. I saw Foster Odom, my lifelong friend, and Marica Brown, my once-girlfriend; saw them standing side-by-side in my mind, like an instant photograph of them caught unaware, standing in a yard, in the evening dusk with a backdrop of trees: both smaller, clean and thin. Foster was tall and skinny, a mop of dirty blonde hair: a keen, hazel stare and sanguine grin frozen forever. He was in jeans and a t-shirt, his elbows bent, his hands shoved confidently into his back pockets as though there wasn't a worry in the world. Marica's gray eyed glance was askance, caught and stilled in a demurred half-blink. A nervous, slanted, wry smile. Her long and red, plaited hair. Her cocked knee. She was a tomboy in a Sunday dress.

I dropped my cigarette on the sidewalk, stepped on it and lit another one on my Zippo. Before me on the busy street, traffic streamed and horns sounded. Someone shot me a bird from a passing car and someone else saluted. I watched the big and bold colored American cars, remembering Foster Odom's blue Shelby Cobra Mustang, my orange SS Camaro, how we used to drag race anyone on the dirt roads back home; wanting to win every time, wanting to own the thrill of speed and power, innately believing we were invincible and reveling in the energy and the moments of the rock music over our car radios--music that neither one of our fathers particularly liked. They preferred a Hank Williams or an Ernie Tubbs. "I can take it up to Elvis," Foster's dad told us once before he died of heat stroke. "But give me Kate Smith."

A male hippie in long, shaggy, dun hair and beard, wearing a teal poncho and leather sandals, came up to me, sneered and spit on my boots. "Like...Napalm, man," his eyes bulged. He nodded at me in fervent agitation. "Like...like..you know, *man!*"

I smoked, narrowed my eyes at him and watched for what he would do. He did nothing but compress his lips in anger, turn and walk away. An elderly couple, holding hands in clean, white and dated clothes, nodded and smiled as they went by. A young mother in a blue midi dress and blonde, page boy hair frowned and steered her child away. Out of the moving crowd of people on the sidewalk, a fair and thin brunette girl with long, dark, frizzled bangs sauntered up to me, barefoot. She was in frayed bell bottoms and wore a cluster of colored glass bead necklaces over a mauve, psychedelic tee shirt. She paused and drew up close to me, staring up into my face with wide, blue, blood-shot eyes and a leering smile, as though I was a curiosity or an artifact. I saw she was stoned and that she wasn't wearing a bra.

"Hey, corporal," she whispered, her breath slow, smoky and sweet. "You kill anybody today?"

"Beat it, kid," I told her.

Her grin fell. She backed off with a shrug and made a peace sign. I watched her breasts bounce as she walked away. I followed her into the streaming crowd with my eyes, smoking and thinking how the bitch didn't know what killing was, didn't know what fear and anger and madness would do to someone. For the memory of Foster this past year, for his friendship, and for something of the belief in the Fermata Bend, Alabama that was in us, I had shot human forms with my M-16 without remorse or a shred of pity. I had killed with my hands, finished off wounded NVA with my bayonet and I had slit Viet Cong guards' throats from behind in the dark with vengeance, muffling their cries of surprise with my other hand, and holding them until they ceased struggling, dying with their eyes open, their blood flowing down their necks, chests and arms to the ground.

I looked after the girl as she moved into the crowd and imagined running up behind her, taking her in front of everyone, and how there wouldn't be a damned thing she could do. I felt the rising surge of my mean glee; the inherent power at the idea, imagined her shocked and startled face as I would come up behind her and grip her throat. *Yeah, sweetie, I'm killing somebody today.* I saw myself holding the razor sharp, ox bone-handled switchblade Vin Trough had given me weeks ago at the Paradise Bar, that was now stuffed somewhere deep in my travel bag. *"From Lao,"* Vin Trough told me, staring at me as she paused between words. *"Doa Lao,"* she said, as if that meant something; her dark, porcine eyes resting rigid and hopeful on me; her slow, bleached smile; her permed, silky black bands and her ever-loud, colored bar dress and high-heeled shoes.

Vin Trough wore thick makeup and smelled of cheap perfume. Like everything else in Vietnam, it seemed, she wasn't real; she was not herself, not a good Vietnamese, nor a good Westerner. She smiled too quick, too much, with her ever-red, painted lips and bleached teeth. She had only known me for a week and from a small room with a gaudy, gilded mirror, a rattan ceiling fan and stuccoed walls layered with taped-on photos of smiling GIs, silk flowers and postcards from other men. *"I want you always safe,"* she said slowly to me with a gradual sigh, when she handed me the knife, her face an instant, sad look of longing beneath the mask. I took it from her hand, palmed it, remembering her room: its smell of heat from the clay roof tiles above, her bed sheets stiff with starch and dried, stale sweat.

"Safe?" I had echoed, giving her a hard grin. *"Safe?"*

Vin Trough could only smile her quick smile. Bleached teeth. Painted lips.

The days and nights blurred from the windows of train passenger cars as I sat, wanting the long way home, in old, bell bottomed jeans, a flannel shirt, socks and loafers; wearing a denim jacket and wire RayBans. I dozed and smoked, ate in the diner car or bought boxed meals. I avoided people and eye contact, spoke to almost no one, only sleeping and gazing out my window for hours in silence at the ever moving scenery of towns and countryside, power lines, trees in slow-changing fall leaves, fields, fences and roads; feeling the incessant rhythm of the train through the gradual and changing terrain. I felt as though I was being reeled back to the beginning in a long, slow film, to what I was not ready to go back to; the incessant and subtle rocking motion pulling and luring old thoughts and even songs from memory--Simon and Garfunkel, for some reason--"The Sound of Silence," "Look for America," "Homeward Bound"; and other songs Foster and I used to listen and sing to, springing from memory, bar for bar, like "Tears of A Clown," "If I Fell," or "It's the End of the World," each song doing repetitions in my head, until another song would come merging, too, into the rhythm of the

train, "Only the Lonely" and "Nights in White Satin," until I
wanted to weep, still seeing the image of Foster Odom in the
sweeping American landscape outside, forever grinning at me,
along with the other dead faces I knew from my platoon; Foster Odom grinning with something of being a Fermata Bend
kid before his Marine haircut; the cocky, fox grin, all tooth
and daring in a thinner frame before the Marines bulked him
up and taught him how to kill people; the blonde mop of hair
over his ears; the keen, willing, hazel stare; but most of all, his
desire to win.

Foster Odom was one of us, and in many ways, he was all
of us boys from Fermata Bend, Alabama, before Vietnam. He
was the male emblem of our Fermata Bend class. He probably thought he could grin the gooks to death and beat them
at their own game, as he did when he snagged a grounder
and threw a runner out from third base or laid a flying hit
on a tailback as a linebacker or as when he stopped to wink
at everyone before taking a foul shot on the basketball court.
He was the only son of Captain Odom, a decorated Marine
in World War Two, who died of heatstroke out in his hayfield
when Foster was nine. From that day forward, Foster had the
curse and the legacy to live up to, more than anyone else. He
had to be worthy, he had to be approved, and he did whatever
it took. He was the first in our age group to kill a buck, the
first to hit a home run, and the first to make Eagle Scout. He
was a Blue Ribbon winner of the FFA Best Steer Competi-
tion. He was President of our class, President of the SGA
and captain of the football team. He was voted Most Likely
to Succeed. He lettered in five sports, was Valedictorian, and
he achieved the highest grade point average ever compiled at
Fermata Bend High School.

Foster, who was the best one of us from Fermata Bend; Foster who grinned; Foster who dared; Foster who led the way. Foster, who was my best friend, who sat in duck or deer binds with me on cold, dawn mornings, who baled hay and mended fences with me in the heat and who drank bootleg beer and sang with me on the railroad tracks. We played baseball and football together. We double-dated, we dragged cars, and we believed in the glory of the music sustained from WLS on our car radios. Growing up in Fermata Bend, our mothers taught us manners, the men taught us how to hunt and play sports. We played war and adventure outside, under the mental aura of those before us who had won The Great War and World War Two. We grew up watching black and white TV shows like *The Grey Ghost*, *Bonanza*, *Combat* and *Twelve O'Clock High*. We grew up with the movies at the Cherokee Drive-In, the likes of John Wayne, Audie Murphy and Robert Mitchum. We grew up listening to Presidents Eisenhower, Kennedy and Johnson on TV; we grew up listening to the veterans and Jared Snead, "The Teller of the Tales," making history larger than life while we stood around and listened at the Co-Op, the post office or the barber shop; the hardware, and around the campfires on coon or fox hunts.

I awoke in the dark with a start, discovering myself alone again in a train seat, my heart pounding, my breathing fast and hard, thinking and feeling as though I had just been with my Ranger platoon, their gaunt, fatigued faces, fanning out helter-skelter from the wind-chopping Hueys into the thick heat and elephant grass and about to wade, holding rifles over our heads, into the muddy Song Vu Gia River. I blinked, recalling the thick heat, scenes of Napalm-scorched earth with smothering and bloated bodies among burnt patches

and charred bamboo frames. I reached and touched the Lao
switchblade Vin Trough had given me in my sock and felt
safe. My pulse and breathing slowed. I recognized the dark
seats around me with sleeping passengers under dimmed,
overhead lights and the incessant, subtle lulling motion of
the train that was taking me home; remembering nights in
the bush in Vietnam, the tense monotony of humping and
securing positions we dubbed "Point Endless"--places with
poor villagers, huts and rice paddies which we took and left
in pursuit of elusive enemy, only to return and take again and
the gray and white Polaroid snapshot Foster's Marine buddy,
a stocky and almost bald Corporal "Pader" from Missouri,
showed me at the commissary in Da Nang when I went there
on two-day leave after learning of Foster's death; after my
mother and Foster's mother wrote me, and after the sudden
influx of letters to me from Fermata Bend; letters from our
teachers, coaches and classmates, the mayor, our minister, the
postman, our girlfriends, town mothers, even the local Garden Club and the UDC; letters written in shock and disbelief
that Foster Odom had been killed in action—written to me
because they could not write to him, and written to me as
though I was the one who could somehow account for it.

    Pader tried to make small talk before he showed me the
gray photo: Foster's shaved and decapitated head impaled on a
bamboo stick, his upturned, glazed-white eyeballs; the tongue
and lower mouth cut out of a bloody, vacuous hole with a
hanging piece of jawbone. I looked away and clamped my
eyes shut. I opened them and tried to breathe.

    "I took it to remember him by," the sad Marine told me.
He gave me an eery grin and told how an NVA sniper had
found Foster's face when he left the patrol to defecate in a
bamboo brake. The patrol didn't find him until much later,

after a firefight and having to call in air strike and artillery. His impaled head and his body was laid out on the ground with his pants and his briefs still dropped down to his knees.

"Nobody wiped his ass," Pader said, shaking his head. "Last time I saw him alive," he informed me, with a slow, morose smile, "Odom said, "Cover me while I shit". . . and then he grinned that grin," Corporal Pader added and shook his head, holding that same eery smile.

I looked away and shook my head when he offered me the snapshot.

"You...you think maybe his parents would want it?" I heard him say.

I shook my head. I couldn't speak. I never wanted to see it again or think of it.

But the photo stayed with me, followed me: an ever harsh and indelible vision of Foster in pale gray, the Marine-shaved head with ghoulish, upturned eyes; the bloody sinew with no mouth. During my second tour for revenge after rage had done its work and I disregarded my promise to Marica-- the photo followed me over and over in reoccurring dreams. The naked, stark reality of the gray photo struck me with a chilling pall, a snapshot in predawn light without color or relief; bland, with no meaning or relevance. My mind raged against that and begged for color. I gave it blue, the color of Foster's old Mustang. My second tour in Vietnam, my rage and the dreams of my memory merged with the memory of that snapshot of death. I made something of the memory of Foster become full and vivid to me, recurring in blue-shaded chiaroscuros. I saw Foster Odom, the daring, strong, good-natured boy from Fermata Bend, Alabama, who did as he was taught and told; who minded his manners and believed in the men. Foster's ghastly, wicked and pallid blue face came to me in my dreams, grinning blue lips and teeth, with startling white, up-turned eyes; dressed in muddy blue, camouflaged jungle fatigues and against a thick blue jungle, a thick, blue Asian night with a palled moon; his surreal, blue, skeleton-grinning face with a blue, hanging jawbone seeming to levitate closer and closer, until each time it stopped and mouthed the words, *You are going to die.*

My blue dreams of Foster came on the hot and sandy road off Nha Trang, as I napped in the back of a Two Ton truck in convoy; they came in the jungle under a half-shelter, north of Qu'Hjon; and on a Monsoon night as I slept on my M-16, draped in my poncho in a downpour on the Plateau du Kontum and my visions of an unmaimed Foster Odom came, too, him living in blue: him grinning beside the blue Shelby Cobra Mustang back home, then; in blue jeans, blue plaids, blue corduroys; in blue football uniform, blue baseball and basketball uniforms; in his blue formal at the last high school prom...and in his Marine Blues.

Other nights, I dreamed of Fermata Bend, feeling Foster's familiar presence but without Foster in sight. I saw the veterans much aged and white-haired; my father, bald and wizen-faced; Jared Snead, thin, feeble and bowed over in baggy clothes with a long, white-beard touching the ground, like a caricature of Rip Van Wrinkle or a picture of an old Civil War veteran, while all the now aged hometown veterans stood together in a small circle in a wind storm in the Fermata Bend town cemetery, the slow *plinking* of the keys from Beueregard's piano whirling in the wind and the men hovering in their circle among the worn and weathered tombstones and statuettes, among the old oaks and the cedars. They held their faces up, then in soiled trench coats and helmets, and grinning in some kind of cocky comradery, then they stretched their arms out together in unison while spirits of the home town cemetery rose up about them, heads first and like mists through the graves; history I once knew, the people I knew of; and the people I never knew but had been told about all my life; Fermata Bend spirits raining skyward up and above the aging veterans and Jared Snead's heads, like slow shades dressed in their times, heads bowed and gazing down; faces blissful, serene and introspective; each one's hands crossed at the waist, as though in public prayer.

I saw them all. I saw founding fathers in full beards, leather boots and rotted dress coats; stern and grim officers in dark hair and dress uniforms with epaulets, Joe Wheeler's haggard Confederates, barefoot in threadbare butternut uniforms with rope-knotted belts; turn-of-the century mayors and merchants in moldy sack suits, bats wing ties and pince-nezes; proper women in fake pearls, piled hair and faded tea gown dresses; young men in dark derbies, moustaches and suits; old women in yellowed white polonaises and ribbon streamers from porkpie hats. I spotted smiling Dough Boys, grimy Rough Riders and Flying Fortress bombardiers. I saw Captain Odom puffed and proud in his World War II dress uniform and my Uncle Bugby grinning in his moldy Eisenhower Jacket, his brimmed hat and spectacles. I saw others from the old, segregated and white cemetery. The dead rose. The dead rose on and on and to a slow *plinking* of piano keys. The dead of my home. The dead of Fermata Bend. The dead rising and looking down.

I watched the dark, rushing world outside my train window turn into gray: empty roads, still fields and houses. I lit another cigarette on my Zippo and stubbed it out in the seat arm ashtray, already filled with my cigarette butts. I sighed, rose in the dim light and sleeping passengers of the gently rocking train, took down my travel bag from the luggage rack above my seat and carried it down the aisle into the Men's Lounge. In the vacant, dingy, white and wire mess tile lounge was a small, corner lavatory and a single ceiling light, a urinal, two wooden stalls and a worn, green Naugahyde couch beneath the chrome railing of a long, frosted window.

I braced my feet against the swaying of the train, laid my travel bag out on the couch and zipped it open. I took out my khaki service uniform on its hanger and hung it on the outside coat hook of the first stall door. I stepped back, lit a cigarette on my Zippo and sat on the end of the bench by the bag, gazing at the hanging uniform and now and then to the entrance door, feeling the rocking motion of the train under my feet, carrying me home to Alabama. No one knew when I was coming. I had not called or written ahead. But even at that, the Fermata Bend veterans, my father, would want me to wear my uniform. *"You boys do us proud, now,"* the town veterans all told us before we left for Vietnam. They nodded and touched our shoulders. Jared Snead swept off his fedora and shook my hand in front of the post office before I left Fermata Bend for the last time, his stare sad. *"I can't tell you,"* he said, shaking his head. *"I can't tell you. But do what they tell you and remember where you came from,"* he paused. *"That will save you."*

I sighed, stubbed my cigarette out in the bench's chromed arm ashtray, rose and removed my toilet kit from my travel bag and set it on the window ledge above the porcelain lavatory. I stripped out of my shirt and shaved off a three-day stubble, standing and looking at the wet, hard and gaunt face with its military haircut in the oval mirror. I slapped after-shave on my face, replaced the toilet articles and kit into my travel bag, stripped to my under briefs and t-shirt and slowly put on the uniform on the stall hanger, sitting on the bench to pull on clean socks and shoes from the travel bag and glancing to the entrance door as I slid Vin Trough's switch-blade under my clean, right sock.

I stood, braced my legs akimbo against the swaying of the train and looked into the mirror as I set the Ranger cap on my head, looking into my hard and lean face, looking over the buttons and bars, the tags and stripes. The dark eyes stared back at me, small and barreled. *Me in uniform. Me, Beck Senecal, Army Ranger,* I thought, knowing Foster would never be home again and Marica would not be there to meet me. The lounge entrance door swung open with louder, rocking noise from train outside. A middle-aged, black train porter in a black cap and a white coat barged in. He stopped and stepped back in wide-eyed surprise.

"Oh," he said. "Sorry. You...you scared me...*sir.*"

"Just a corporal," I corrected him with a small smile. "And not even that anymore."

I stepped alone off the passenger car, onto the long concrete platform of the Mobile train station, holding my travel bag and duffel bag under my arms and looked around the milling and chatting people before the familiar stone, three-storey station building; recognizing again the green, overhanging harbor roof and ridge beams; and the weathered, black-on-white *Mobile, AL* signboard hung above the entrance doors. I stood, looked and remembered. The last time I was here, I had not been alone. Marica Brown had kissed me in front of my parents while they stood off with brave smiles in their Sunday clothes and I had promised her to come back. I recalled Marica's gray eyes, the wetness of her kiss, the smell of her skin, Dove soap and Windsong; her urgent hissing of the word into my mouth that vibrated in my teeth--the word I never got. *You will come back,* she said. I remembered saying goodbye to people in town before I left. *Remember where you came from,* I remembered Jared Snead grinning, for some reason, saw him wink. *You give'em hell, boy. Like ole Patton. Like ole Blackjack Pershing would do.*

Standing on the platform with my bags, it now all seemed like a time that never was. I thought how the last time I was on this platform could well have been the last time; the last time on this platform was the last time for the likes of Todd Newman, Curtis Johnson and Foster Odom.

"Hey, soldier," someone spoke.

I turned toward a light mahogany girl in a kinky and golden blonde Afro, smiling at me with ice blue lips and wide gaps in her plain teeth. She wore a dark blue, silk blouse and tight, bright American flag-patterned hot pants.

"You don't remember me?" she drawled. She looked hurt. She made a nervous laugh.

I searched her face. "Dea?" I said, disbelieving. "Dea Banes?"

She nodded slowly with relief. Dea had the same brown eyes. She had bright gold jewelry on her ears, wrists and neck. She had a wide, white belt in the loops of her hot pants and she had a white leather, fringed handbag hanging off her shoulder on string straps.

"Dea," I said. "Dea...you're...*blonde*," I blurted out.

"Oh...yeah," she smiled. She shrugged and laughed. She came forward and hugged me. I dropped my bags.

"Oh, Beck," Dea cried into my shoulder. "Oh, Beck," she said, and began to cry. It took a moment for me to put my arms around her.

"I came for you," Dea cried, her voice rising and shrill. "I came for you," she said, "cause I knew nobody else would."

"You came for me?" I echoed. She nodded into my shoulder and began sobbing. White people passed and looked at us twice. I tried to see her face. I didn't have a handkerchief. I parted from her, motioning for her to wait. I knelt, unzipping my travel bag on the concrete platform and found an olive-drab, army tee shirt.

"Here," I said, rising and thrusting it on her. I shook it. "Just here."

Her mouth had curved down at the corners and her tears were streaking thick mascara down her cheeks. She shook her head but took the tee shirt. Dea wiped her eyes, blew her nose, still crying. She slowly folded the tee shirt and offered it back.

"Er, no. You keep it," I said.

"Oh, Beck," Dea shook her head. She bunched up the tee shirt in her hands and wiped her nose on it. "Jared Snead's died," she sniffed. "Foster Odom, Curtis Johnson and Todd Newman all came home in caskets. And Bubba Smith is Missing in Action," she said.

I nodded, could only stare. Dea was blonde, dressed loud. She was wearing a gold, rope necklace; gold-stemmed, white balled earrings and she had long, white fingernails. Out of an old and reflective Fermata Bend habit with women, I remembered to take my cap off.

"How?" I said. "How did you…?"

Dea made a sad laugh; her big, welled-up eyes staring me in. "Oh," she doffed the balled-up tee shirt away from us in her hand. "I got ways, baby." She sniffed and forced a smile, sweeping her free and nervous hand over her blonde hair.

"I had a hunch, baby," she said. "Called the congressman's office and acted like your white relative." Dea laughed. "Army said you'd left, but the airlines said you didn't. So, I checked the train lines and the arrival times, started making guesses and driving down to wait."

"Wait?" I said. "You drove down to wait?"

"What were you going to do?" Dea play-pouted.. "Not tell your parents and take the bus?"

I nodded and stared at her, remembering how Foster and I hunted the river bottomland with her younger brother, Edmond. Hunting boots, overalls and long-sleeved shirts; crisp air and the smell of discharged shotgun shells among dead leaves. Edmund grinned with a missing tooth. We sometimes gave Edmond and Dea rides to and from town on the dirt roads. Sometimes we took canned goods and used clothes from our parents and left them on their father's, Beersheba's wooden porch. In high school, Dea wore plain, limp dresses; short, kinky, black hair; black sunglasses and sandals. She carried a large, dog-eared Bible like a badge of authority, quoting from it and clutching it to her breasts as if for protection while she argued civil rights and the need for brotherly and sisterly love.

"Dea," I said. "Dea, why are you here?"

Dea gave me a still, wet stare. Her blonde Afro, her clothes and mascara-smeared cheeks.

"Because," she said.

"Because?"

She shrugged. "Yeah...because," Dea said, looking off, matter-of-fact. She balled up the army tee shirt in her hands. "Because, it was all I could do," she said.

"Was it Marica?" I asked, speaking a sudden thought, seeing her gray eyes and red hair.

"No, it ain't Marica," Dea said. "You broke her heart."

I couldn't say anything to that. Dea nodded and tried a smile, but the corners of her mouth turned down and her eyes filled. She came forward and hugged me hard, clutching my tee shirt.

"Oh, Beck," Dea declared. "Beck," she cried beside my ear, as if I understood how she felt; as if that and the fact we were all from Fermata Bend explained everything.

While Dea walked, she kept my tee shirt balled up in her hands, chattering nonstop and glancing back to me, her voice high and nervous as I followed her into the train station parking lot with my bags.

"I made sure to come get you and not tell anyone, baby," Dea informed me. "In case that's how you wanted it...it's nothing to do with Marica," she repeated. "I left the real estate office this morning on personal leave and drove to Mobile...took a wrong turn while someone called Bill Withers sang long and slow on the radio about 'Ain't No Sunshine'."

Dea laughed, nervous, as though wanting relief. She called me "baby". She told me how she had sold two black peoples' houses and a small farm last week and had also driven alone to see the Carpenters concert in New Orleans. She wanted to see *Love Story* and *The Last Picture Show,* if she got the chance. She wanted to see the group, America. While she talked, she kept glancing to me with quick smiles, touching her blonde Afro.

I tried not to watch her slender back and waist, the firm orbs of her ass swiveling in her bright American Flag patterned hot pants. I nodded and listened, still wondering what she was doing here, beginning to understand that talking was less awkward for her than silence, and recalling Edmond, Dea's brother, in his worn overalls, hunting coat and boots, and then Beersheba, their father, who would stand large and bareheaded and gray in his worn overalls and boots, too, on the gray boards of the porch of their weathered tenant shack embossed in scuppernong vines whenever Foster and I might drop off food from our parents during the holidays or take Edmund home in one of our hot rods or one of our parents' trucks after hunting, leaving our kill on the porch for Beersheba who would always smile with his few and yellowed teeth, and nod and laugh at whatever we said, even if it wasn't funny; his manner servile, calling us "Mr. Foster" and "Mr. Beck". I saw Dea back there then: thin as a stick, in something like an old, thin dress and pigtails, staring us in

from behind a tattered screen door: large eyes without a sound.
And then I thought of my mother and father and grinned at
the thought of their surprised and beaming faces and the way
they might look at me, with some awe or pride. Only, I was not
ready. I was not ready to go back.

"And how was the trip, baby?" Dea interrupted herself, glancing at me with a quick smile, and then avoiding my gaze. "Hey, I
talk too much, don't I?"

She forced a laugh. I smiled, recognizing the softness of
her drawl that was both black and Fermata Bend, Alabama. I
stopped with Dea at a white, recent model, two-door Lincoln
that was parked off-angle in a parking space, its soft convertible
top folded down. The front grill and the wheels were chrome.
The interior was bright white. On the outside of the door, printed in bold purple was the line: *Pecan Tree Real Estate 288-1103.*

"Here we be," Dea declared. "I sell real estate now." She
sighed, turned to me and smiled, padding my balled up tee shirt
in her hands. I nodded for her, noting the gaps in her teeth, the
blonde hair and her dried, mascara-smeared cheeks.

"Real estate, huh?" I said.

Dea shrugged. "Mr. Hubbard got me specializing in black
folks, cause he can't ... or won't," she stated. "Rich land and poor
blacks," Dea quipped. "What we got the most of in Fermata
Bend."

I nodded and smiled, looking over the door sign; the large,
white-walled tires; the chromed wheels.

"Dea," I said, turning to her, "why are you here?"

She didn't answer. I paused. "Where's Edmond?" the
thought came to me.

Dea made a slow and sad smile, her eyes welling up.

"He's over there, too," she said, matter-of-fact. "He followed
all you white boys chasing your daddies' glory."

I thought I understood then.

"I'm sorry," I said. "I wish him luck."

"I get letters from him with muddy finger prints," Dea stared at me, fear creeping into her voice. "And they don't... they don't really say anything."

"What's his outfit?"

"The First Cav."

I nodded and tried to smile. "I wish him luck," I said.

"Yeah," Dea huffed her breath. "Wish him luck."

She tried to smile, too, and she looked away. "I drove Jared Snead to all the boys' funerals," she told me. "I stood with him and what seemed like everybody from Fermata Bend while the honor guards shot the twenty-one gun salutes, played taps and laid the caskets in the ground, except Foster," she said, looking at me. "Foster's momma placed him in a tomb in her back yard, alongside his daddy. His momma wanted him there instead of Arlington," Dea explained. She paused.

"But all Fermata Bend was there," her voice went soft. "All Fermata Bend was in the Odom's back yard." Her eyes widened and blinked as though she was still in disbelief. "And everyone wept," she said with a pause. "Everyone wept."

Dea tried to smile, dabbed her eyes with my balled-up tee shirt in her hands. She sniffed, looked at me and stood there clutching the balled-up tee shirt, until I realized she was waiting on me.

"Oh," I said, remembering my old Fermata Bend manners. I dropped both of my bags, stepped forward and opened the driver's door.

"Thank *you*," Dea said. She smiled then, clutching the balled up tee shirt and slid into the white bucket seat behind the white dash and the white steering wheel, slipping the string purse off of her shoulder. I shut her door, hefted my bags into the back seat, went around the car, opened the front passenger door and got in, too. As I shut the door, Dea tried to hold her smile, but she looked off over the steering wheel and bit her lip. She shut her eyes and began to cry, reaching for my tee shirt in her lap, wiping her face on it, her mascara almost gone now.

"I'm sorry," she sniffed.

I nodded and thought to touch her.

"I just can't believe it," she said. "I can't believe it."

I nodded. "I know," I said.

After a few moments, Dea took a deep breath. She sniffed and smiled. She dropped my tee shirt in her lap, reached to the dash, pushed open the car's ashtray, took out a finely rolled joint and offered it to me. I stared at it in her long, dark hand with her white-painted nails.

The idea of doing it with her wasn't comfortable. I shook my head no. She made a closed smile and shrugged. She replaced the joint in the ashtray, closed it, reached behind my bucket seat and lifted the lid to a small, plastic cooler on the rear floorboard. She fished out a dripping gold can of Michelob from the ice and held it out to me with a grin.

"Oh, okay," I smiled. "Okay."

"Cheers, soldier," Dea's voice quavered. But she smiled as if she wanted to party, as if we had partied once before.

I took the can from her, brought it down below the dash and held it at my knees. "Thank you, Dea," I said, nodding. "Thank you for coming to get me."

Dea smiled and watched me as I pulled the tab ring and took a swallow. The cold, numbing beer hit the back of my throat. I gasped. Tears swelled to my eyes. Dea laughed, took the car keys out of the purse beside her in the seat and started the engine. The car's headers boomed, filled and settled into an old and familiar droning, like Foster's hot rod and my hot rod used to do.

I took another swallow and grinned at her. "You're not drinking?" I said.

Dea frowned and shook her head. "Reputation," she said. "I'm in real estate now."

I looked at her and laughed. It seemed silly, funnier than it was.

The tires squealed and the Lincoln lurched forward as Dea turned the car out of the train station parking lot onto the road. I gripped the door rest with my free hand and stared ahead, tucked the beer can between my knees and reached for my seat belt. She shot me a grin, driving fast, braking and weaving the large, convertible Lincoln through the traffic and stop lights, onto the Mobile Airport Road and toward the Interstate.

Slow down, I tried to utter to her, staring at the road. The words caught in my throat. I swept off my Ranger cap, gripping the beer can in one hand and the door rest in the other. I discovered myself muttering, *Slow down, Slow down,* but my words were swallowed in the wind hitting me over the windshield of the car and the rolled-down windows. I looked to Dea but she only grinned and glanced at me, as though everything was okay, her mouth moving, saying something I couldn't hear. I stared at her large, gapped teeth, her light mahogany face with its dried, mascara-smeared cheeks and her loud blonde Afro, saw it as a face belonging to some naive, foolhardy kid. *This can not be happening,* I thought. *I can not be here.*

I stared ahead as the Lincoln sped onto the bypass, onto I-65 North, the long car surging smoothly into the traffic, moving between the lanes. Dea's mouth opened into a wide, silent laugh. She began to yell above the wind in her

black and Fermata Bend drawl about things that seemed irrelevant and bizarre, something about a blue ceramic flowerpot
on the outside ledge of her bedroom window, a new movie
she saw called "Carnal"-something and the latest episode of
something called *All In the Family*.

I could only stare at her moving mouth and then at the
road, feeling as if I were being transported in a daze, wondering if she was crazy, and then recalling the speed--the same
kind of reckless, thrilling speed Foster and I used to drive our
hotrods in, with our sure and cocky grins, our longer hair and
paisley shirts; our flared jeans and dingo boots, dragging off
the stop lights or on the back river roads, squealing our tires
while we spun up dust. Above the wind, I caught something
from Dea about a new Polaroid camera, a band called "All
man"-something.

"Really, really cool," Dea trilled at me in the wind. She
grinned. I gaped at her. I nodded and stared.

After awhile, the only thing to do was to catch my breath,
look away from her and at something else, look at the barren,
rust-colored fields and the hardwoods with the colorful, turning leaves of an Alabama November; to breathe the cool wind
and try to remember that I, too, was like her in a carefree way
once, that I was from here and a part of this place; and try
to comprehend that I was truly back, while boys like Bubba
Smith were MIA and others like Foster Odom, Todd Newman and Curtis Johnson were now dead. I stared out from
the car in the wind and gulped the beer, feeling both grateful
and guilty that I was alive to drink it, thinking how my father's face would light up with pride and confidence when he
saw me again; my mother's face would be tearful and relieved
and it would show strain, like in her constant stream of letters
to me in Vietnam. *All Fermata Bend Mourns,* my mother had

scribbled on the edge of Foster's obituary. *One of our best is laid to rest.* Mother had underlined the clippings where it told of Foster Odom's Fermata Bend family history, like the more recent clipping she had sent along of Old Man Jared Snead, the clipping told of Foster's mother, his deceased father, the Captain; his distant kinship to Jared Snead; his grandparents, great-grandparents, and great-great grandparents, like almost everyone who had Pecan Family in Fermata Bend, along with his outstanding attributes as an athlete, a leader and a scholar; a member of the Fermata Bend First Methodist Church, an Eagle Scout from Troop 147, a blue ribbon winner in the FFA, president of his high school class, captain of the football team, a Merit Scholar, Valedictorian, and a member of Boys State.

In Vietnam, I had envisioned everyone from Fermata Bend standing together in a gray rain, solemn, stunned and dressed in black, among the cedars and the dull, stained tombstones of townspeople and soldiers in the old town cemetery: Andrew Jackson's men, Confederates, Rough Riders, World War One, World War Two and Korean War soldiers. I had wept, too, at Foster's death, and raged at the loss of it all, and had signed on for the second tour to avenge my loss, Fermata Bend's loss on the Charlies. But in the end, there was nothing for it, no resolution, and nothing to show. Other than a sense of having purged my feelings, I was right back where I had started. *Damn you, Beck Senecal,* Marica had written me. *Damn you.*

I looked at Dea, her strangeness, her dried, mascara-tinted cheeks, her large eyes on the road and her lips still moving, as though talking to herself. The wind pressed her blonde Afro back into a slant as she drove. She caught my stare. Her lips stopped. She gave me a relaxed, abashed smile. The car slowed.

"Sorry," she drawled above the wind. "Am I talking your ears off?"

I stared at her, remembering to smile and to shake my head no, but feeling the ever Disconnect, looking at her, that I had begun to feel in Nam. Dea grinned. She turned on the car radio. A loud song with heavy bass blared on about "Maggie" something.

"What is that?" I yelled at her above the wind, the radio.

"That?" Dea yelled, turning her eyes to me from the road. "Oh, hey, baby. That's Rod Stewart."

"Rod who?"

It ended and another song blared on I didn't know. I listened. Then another came on. "Cat Stevens," Dea said. Then, "Jim Croce." Dea gave me quizzical grins each time.

"Oh," I said and nodded.

"Why don't you listen to Soul?" I yelled above the wind, the radio, remembering Edmond, how he hummed The Supremes, James Brown and Marvin Gaye.

Dea frowned, turning her eyes on the road. She shrugged. "I only like white music, now, baby," she yelled back.

I looked at Dea and saw her as strange. I shook my head, gulped the last of the beer, tucked the can between my legs, ducked toward the floorboard and lit a cigarette on my Zippo.

"James Taylor," Dea said, her voice gleeful as I straightened up, cupping the cigarette in my hand, drawing on it against the wind as another song came on. I nodded, smoked and listened. It was slow, smooth and sad, about fire and rain.

"That one's nice," I said and smoked.

A farmer's weather report blared on, a Breck Shampoo commercial, an announcement of the time, and then an old, familiar song by The Doors. That reminded me Jim Morrison was dead.

"Geez, Beck," Dea called out with a teasing grin after she told me the next song was "Country Roads," by a John Denver. "Didn't y'all keep up with radio over there?"

I stared at her easy, gapped smile, feeling a sudden well of anger. *Stupid bitch,* I thought, taking in her smooth, ignorant face; the dried, mascara-tinted cheeks and the tight, kinky, blonde hair pressed back by the wind while she drove a big white convertible. I saw PFC Harmon's grimed hands rise and fall after his head was blown off in fine, bloody spray, before his muddied, uniformed carcass took a slow step and fell.

You think I had time to give a shit about radio?

Dea's look fell. I watched her make a nervous laugh and avert her eyes. I watched her stare waver on the road ahead. She swallowed, gripping the steering wheel. The Lincoln picked up speed, the sound from the radio seeming to mix, rise and fall in the increased wind. I sat there in the front passenger's seat and watched her begin to twirl and tug on the end of her gold rope necklace with her nervous hand. I watched how the tight line of the necklace pressed against her neck. *Like a noose,* I thought, and remembered the honed, sharp switchblade that Vin Trough had given me was in my sock; how I could draw that same line with the blade across her neck, if I wanted to--so quick and smooth she wouldn't know what hit her--as I had done to wounded VC after fire fights, to more than one Viet Cong guard on night raids and all for the memory of Foster Odom.

"So, er--so, er," Dea suddenly stammered, her voice loud above the wind. "I-I guess you been out of it, huh?" She gave a high, quavering laugh. She swallowed, holding her unsteady stare on the road. She tugged her necklace hard and fast.

I stared at her and offered no response. *You can die,* I thought, as an answer. *You can die and rot and your life doesn't mean shit.*

"So, you--you glad to be home?" she uttered, trying something against my silence.

I blinked, remembered Marica. *You are going to carry me across the threshold?* she had said. *You want me to cook your meals and darn your socks?* I sighed and I shook my head no. There was no reason to be glad. I discovered the cigarette in my hand and took a draw.

Dea uttered something else, but I didn't hear. I looked to the dash and windshield of the speeding Lincoln, thinking I should throw Vin Trough's knife away before I forgot where I was. I was once again in a bright and fast American car, on an American highway with the radio on. I looked at Dea, her face and clothes and hair, her unaffected attitude. I could almost remember, I could almost be there. I uttered a hard laugh, reached forward and snapped off the irritating noise of the radio. I looked away at the autumn woods of Alabama, feeling a sneer on my face as I smoked and we rode on.

"Are you, er...okay now?" Dea tittered, shooting me a wary look and letting the gold rope necklace drop off her finger. I turned to her. She stared at the road, gripping the wheel with both hands, and began talking nonstop above the wind, without the radio now, in a rapid, forced and loud cheerfulness--for herself, I realized, for her fear. I caught something about a Liza Minnelli movie; a new, plastic Bic cigarette lighter and a new chrome Spiro Agnew wristwatch. Snickers candy bars and a drink called Fresca. I could only stare at her and nod, as though I understood.

"Aren't you glad to be home?" Dea said, her look on me, her expression incredulous. She turned her eyes back to the road, chanced another look at me.

I smoked and didn't answer.

"But you're from here," Dea said, as if that answered it. "You're one of us."

Dea turned the Lincoln off the Interstate onto the exit toward Fermata Bend, slowing into the two-lane county road with weed-choked ditches on either side and the familiar run of rusted barbed wire fences before pastures, pine thickets, farm houses and long stretches of bare, grey pecan orchards. I was back in the fertile, rural bottomland between the Tombigbee and Escatawpa Rivers, dull autumn fields, thick hardwoods and pine thickets. We went slowly down the two-lane and into Fermata Bend in almost no traffic, past Joe Austin's overgrown used-car lot and Elvin Mort's Texaco filling station, going around the small, circular town square past city hall and the bricked, two-storey buildings around the Confederate statue in the center median with weathered flags on two flagpoles and the World War One artillery piece beside the marble Veterans' Obelisk.

"Welcome back," Dea offered. "You-you want to stop?"

I shook my head no and Dea drove on around the square, past Brown's Drug Store where Marcia and I used to park at the curb in my Camaro and talk, where Foster and I used to peddle our bikes to as kids, read comics or eat ice cream cones on the front steps, listen to the old-timers and watch traffic go by. Past the square, Dea drove slowly through the two green lights, by the post office, the Co-Op and then along the white, framed houses with clapboard porches, cracked sidewalks and old oaks in the yards. We passed the white, wood-framed, turn-of-the century Veterans' Lodge, peeling and in need of paint. I thought of the endless monotony of jungle, huts and rice paddies in Vietnam. I thought of Jared Snead, "The Teller of the Tales," grinning with old teeth, sitting on a fence in his worn hunting coat and brown fedora. I saw him in his cleaned, grandfather's formal at the Veterans'

Ball. I heard the slow *plinking* of piano keys and I remembered Foster dancing with his mother and then his girlfriend,
Abbie Stewart, all in their in formals, too, over the heart-pine
floorboards and before the blazing fireplace of the armory,
below the mounted deer heads, the old general's sword in its
scabbard on the mantle and the row of dusty, stern soldiers'
faces looking on from photographs and daguerreotypes along
the walls. I tried to imagine what was left of Foster's face now
in the still and the dark of the tomb in his mother's back yard,
the body rotting in its Marine Blues. I imagined myself coming back, too, in a plastic body bag and then in a metal casket
with an honor guard to Fermata Bend, Alabama; another boy
from here who had been brought up to do what his father,
his town and his country had expected of him, not knowing
anything about reasons or Vietnam.

"You're quiet," Dea said. She braked at the edge of town
for an old woman to cross the street. The frail, white woman
in a plain house dress, high heels and thick glasses began to
smile and wave, then on a double take, gave us a hard look
and a scowl as she crossed. I didn't know if I knew her. Two
farmers went by us in a pickup truck. They waved. In small
town South, that was habit.

"I said...you're quiet," Dea spoke, cheerful, dismissing the
woman. I didn't answer. She turned her eyes back to the road
and drove on and braked at the last stop light before the road
ran on as county highway out of town and toward my parents'
home, the interminable, two-lane stretch through farmland,
etched forever in my memory. But it was new blacktop now,
with bright orange lines through the expanse of the same
pecan orchards, pastures and woods, where Foster and I had
ridden horses, the school bus, peddled our bicycles, raced our
hotrods, and had run every summer on foot to get in shape.

I glimpsed his grinning face in the limelight of the dash behind the white steering wheel of his blue, Shelby Cobra Mustang; and glimpsed Foster revving the engine on a warm, summer night, before squealing his tires off this stop light; his radio blaring "Born to be Wild" or "Can't Get No Satisfaction".

I looked at Dea. "Would you recognize me?" I said.

"Huh?" Dea gave me a startled frown.

I stared at her, her hair, her clothes, her bright, loud presence in the car, realizing I would not have recognized her, either.

"Oh," Dea drawled. "Oh, yeah, baby, sure," she nodded. She kept nodding. She hesitated, her eyes filled. She shook her head no. She tried to smile. I thought of what Marica once was, Foster, and then Edmond, who was over there now. I thought of Jared Snead, who made legend truth, led our fathers and the veterans in the telling of the tales at the hardware, the Co-Op, or the barbershop; his wizened face and unkempt beard; his old-teeth smile and limp fedora; "The Teller of the Tales," as the men referred to him; the old man who led the hunts, led the Veterans' Day Parade and was emcee of the Veterans' Ball; always obsequious and polite, sweeping off his fedora for the women and nodding for the men.

I watched Dea bite her lip, the corners of her mouth curling down. She wiped her eyes on the back of each of her hands, alternating her grip on the steering wheel as she began to cry now as she did at the train station and our talk of Edmund. We sat there, mute in the car, and we didn't move. The stoplight changed to yellow, red, then green.

"We were just kids once, Dea," I offered. "We were just kids."

Dea nodded--too fast, too quick--as though she could pretend to understand, as though to agree was the only thing to do. She shoved the car's transmission lever into park, took up my army tee shirt that had remained beside her in her bucket seat. She brought it up to her face with both hands and began to sob.

I stared at her and could not feel anything, could not think of a thing to say. The knife was in my sock and I didn't have a handkerchief. I thought to touch her, her strangeness now; but I hesitated, couldn't bring myself to do it. All I could think to do was reach down and turn on the radio. A loud, slow and upbeat song about "We've only just begun" blared on and finished while Dea sobbed, a song that I had not heard, or that I could not remember. A cheerful commercial voice came on about Ban Roll On deodorant, then a regional voice came on about Buffalo Rock Root Beer, and then a low, matter-of-fact voice came on and gave the local weather report. *Cloudy skies and mild temperatures,* the voice hummed. *High today sixty-two. Low tonight thirty-four. Chance of rain twenty percent. Tomorrow will change for a nicer day, sunny and cool with a projected high of sixty-nine and a low of thirty-eight. Stayed tuned for more....*

I stared at Dea as we sat before the lone traffic light and she cried into my tee shirt, in the sound of the radio, the music and words becoming irrelevant noise, the stoplight persistently and slowly changing colors: red, yellow, green; yellow, red; yellow, green. A farmer's heavy truck rumbled up and braked behind us, it honked and drove around us through a green light. Two cars followed, each one braking and going around us, too. But we continued to sit unmoving in the idling car and the sound of the radio before the long stretch of what was once familiar road, now covered in new blacktop.

Everything seemed to become timeless. I stared at Dea crying, felt the wind touching my hair, heard the radio sound-

ing, knowing that the stoplight was slowly and forever changing colors. Then I touched her and wanted to, reaching for
her strangeness, her hand, on my side of the bunched-up tee
shirt at her face. I took her hand and brought it down to the
console between our seats, holding it in mine like I would
have with a white girl on a Saturday night from Fermata
Bend just a few years ago. Dea let me hold it. She squeezed
my hand back and continued crying into the tee shirt that
she held to her face with the other hand. I looked down at
our interlocked hands and then I looked up and stared at
her—her face and blonde Afro--then, abruptly, Dea, sniffed,
dropped my tee shirt into her lap, yanked her hand free
from me and shoved the transmission lever into drive with a
resolved and tear-stained face. She gripped the steering wheel
hard in both hands, stepped on the gas and drove us through
a yellow light.

I looked away then and closed my eyes, smelling the old,
familiar earth and the cool brush of the November air on my
face. I tried not to think, still knowing and seeing the rolling
land: fields, pecan orchards, hardwoods and pines ahead of
us. I could feel the absence of others and the presence of the
car. I could feel Dea's presence, her hard and hurt silence; I
could hear the garbled radio as the car surged ahead smooth
and fast, and I wondered how many moments had gone down
this road.

Later, I seemed to come to, as though coming out of a fog; to recognize that I was sitting in one of the twin, green wingback chairs on the oak floor of the living room of my home, across from my parents, seated on the coach and watching me with attentive and teary faces; to recognize that I was among the Belgian rugs and dark furniture and the front double windows with their thick, opened drapes, this, after I had seen and heard my mother cry and my father shout in the yard; after they had come running out of the house to the sound of the two pointers barking; after I had dropped my bags on the rock macadam walk and we hugged and laughed and cried, the pointers circling us, wagging their tails and barking. "Hey, soldier!" my father declared over and over. "Hey, soldier!" He was in faded work overalls and a flannel shirt, his baseball cap knocked off onto the ground, his thin hair disheveled, a relieved smile spreading wrinkles over his weathered face like a spider web. My mother reached up and pulled off my Ranger cap and took my face into her hands, shushing the pointers and laughing. "My boy's come home!" she cried. "My boy's come home!" Her worried, weary look.

She was in a plain house dress and apron.   Her steel hair was pinned back, limp and close to her head.   Her eyes brimmed tears, squinted deep crows' feet.

That was after Dea had turned off the highway, too, and then braked hard when I told her to, the Lincoln's tires grinding into the thin chert of the drive that cut through the pasture toward my parents' rock house among the yellowing leaves of the sweet gums.   She blinked at me and hesitated when I told her I wanted to walk the last bit alone.   She forced a smile, watching me with her tired, red eyes from crying and her mascara-smeared face as I set my Ranger cap on my head, slowly got out of the Lincoln on the front passenger side and shut the door.   I lifted my bags out of the back seat. I looked at her and remembered my manners.

"Thanks, Dea," I nodded.   "Thanks for bringing me home."

"It wasn't Marica," she said with a closed smile.

"It's not you," I said at her blank look.   "I need to do this," I nodded, not being able to explain how Foster and I used to talk about coming home, walking down our own home paths as boys turned into men, as though in an old black and white war movie.   We imagined parades, too, like the annual Veterans' Day Parade always led by Jared Snead, everyone in Fermata Bend waving and smiling at us as we marched around the town square; like the homecoming parades the World War One and WW II veterans talked about. We wanted the Fermata Bend veterans to smile and be proud of us.   We wanted to be American victors, too.

And that was after I stood there and Dea said, "Well...I know.   You need to see your parents alone.   They don't need to see me right now," she laughed, and then, "Hey, hey, your shirt," reaching and holding up the rumbled army tee shirt from her lap.   I smiled and told her to keep it.

"Wash it and wear it with some worn jeans," I said.

She lowered the tee shirt, pursed her lips and fixed her red eyes on me then, swallowing as though trying to get up the courage to say something. I stood there with my bags while she got out of the Lincoln, leaving the driver's door open and the engine idling, and came around the front of the car. I watched her watching me with a tentative grin. She swallowed, quickly placed her hands on my shoulders and kissed me.

"If you can't have Marica, you can have me," she whispered, her eyes shifting away as she parted.

I understood then why she was at the train station. I looked at her face and eyes and I thought of how things had changed. I thought of Vin Trough and how both she and Dea kissed alike, both desperate and wanting something. Before Vietnam, I would never have thought of kissing a black girl or a Vietnamese girl, or any girl, other than one like Marica. But now, it all seemed alike. It was all right.

Dea stepped away and smiled. "Well...bye, baby," she offered.

I nodded. "Bye," I said.

She looked back at me as she went around the car, got in behind the wheel and shut the driver's door. She looked at me from behind the wheel and her smile fell.

"Pray for Edmond," she said.

I nodded. "I wish him luck."

And after Dea then spun the big Lincoln around in the grass of the pasture and back onto the chert drive towards the highway. "Ta-ta," she called, with her blonde Afro, her mascara-smeared face and the gaps in her teeth, doffing her hand in a casual wave as she drove away. "Be seeing you. Be good," she said.

And after I had turned and walked on alone, like in a slow dream, feeling Foster's absence now, more than ever, feeling the absence of everything and only me--walking down the chert drive through the pasture, under a gray sky and toward the old rock house, carrying my bags past the white-painted, wood fence and into the still yard and the macadam walk, and then to my parents' shouting and their running from the house, while the pointers barked at me and wagged their tails.

After I hugged my father and kissed my mother, and my father and I waited until she stopped crying, the one who knocked off my cap and touched my face and wanted me home again; the one who had written the letters as though I would come home again, Foster or no Foster, Johnny New-man, Curtis Johnson, or Bubba Smith; the one who wrote the letters full of belief that we would all return to the world as she knew it, Fermata Bend. Dad and I waited on her and after more hugs and my dad's grins, the dogs still barking, my parents' loud voices and laughter ringing in my ears, they herded me inside; my father carrying my bags to my bed in the bedroom that seemed smaller and otiose and just the same as I had left it two years ago. I tossed my cap onto my desk, before the dresser and the mirror; the bookshelves with the stacked albums and the stereo, and the same teenage photos and posters along the wall. I turned around and laughed with my mom and dad as they stood watching me in the doorway to my old room. And as we turned and walked back out together, Dad, who was never one to say much, gave me a quick, teary look and touched my arm, as though to be sure that I was there.

In one of the two green, wingback chairs of the living room, I slowly smoked in front of my parents, something I had never done before, flicking the ashes into my grandfather's old crystal ashtray on the side reading table, my mother and father's flushed, grinning faces facing me from where they sat on the couch. They seemed tired, wrung out with something like exhausted relief, leaning toward me now and then, their grins going to closed smiles and back to grins. My mother clasped and unclasped her hands. She dabbed her eyes on her apron, spreading and re-spreading it over the lap of her dress. My father's grin was proud, solemn and relieved. He watched me, eyed my uniform, now leaning back, now leaning forward and resting his crossed forearms on his knees. I recognized my parents' voices, fielded their many and short questions with polite and short answers. Nothing important. Nothing that mattered. They nodded and smiled at whatever I said. They nodded when I didn't say anything.

"I wanted to surprise you," I answered their question. I nodded after them. "My footlockers are being shipped."

But now, that didn't matter, either. I was home. I watched my mother and father nod and smile, their eyes on me. Beyond them, I recognized the opened French doors that led into the dining room, to the dark Persian rug and the dining table beneath the portrait of my great-grandfather, my mother's grandfather, in butternut uniform above the mantel of the fireplace: that stern face, that black beard and the dark, haunting eyes that had followed me all of my life. I could ignore him now. I smiled and chatted with my mother and father, trying to act casual and relaxed. When I remembered the switchblade in my sock, it didn't seem to belong.

"You're home. You're home," my mom said.

She wiped her eyes with her hands and my dad touched her back. They looked at me with grateful smiles. Mom rose. "And I'm going to fix your old favorite," she declared with a laugh. I nodded and smiled for her, but for a second I couldn't remember what my favorite dish was.

"Chicken and dumplings?" I said.

Mom nodded and got teared-up. "I'm so—" her voice broke. "I'm so grateful," she managed.

I gave her a smile and a nod. "I'm home, mom."

Dad grinned at me from the couch. "Everyone's going to be glad to see you, Beck," he said. "Everyone."

"Oh, yes," Mom said. "I want you to wear that uniform, too, when we go to church...when we get to see your cousins." She smiled. "I want to show you off."

I smiled and nodded. Mom squeezed my shoulder as she went around my chair, toward the kitchen.

Dad watched me from the couch. "Beck," he gave me a sad smile, "you heard about Jared Snead?"

"Jared Snead," I said, nodding. "Yeah," I managed. "I heard, Dad. It's too bad."

Dad nodded. "Me and the boys—we've decided to honor him on Veterans' Day," he informed me. "Have a vigil at his grave after the march." He made a solemn nod and grin. "Now, you can join us," he said.

I tried to smile for him. "Yeah, Jared Snead," I said. "March," I nodded. I kept nodding and began to feel The Disconnect.

After dinner in the dining room and under my grand-father's portrait, I smoked and glanced to the same eyes and rapt faces of my parents while we sat on the sofa in the dark family room, watching *The Brady Bunch* and *Hawaii Five-0* on the black and white TV, recalling how I, too, watched that TV here with Foster, or at his house, the Saturday night westerns and war movies, the summer action re-runs; how Foster and I grew up watching prime time shows like *Combat!, Twelve O'Clock High, The Gallant Men* or *Blue Light*. In the middle of an Ajax detergent commercial, I stubbed my cigarette out in my grandfather's crystal glass ashtray mother had placed on the side table for me. I rose and walked into the light casting off the TV, turned around and smiled down at my parents.

"Foster is dead," I stated to them, as if to confirm the unspoken fact. I stood before their surprised faces, the TV to my back, and I watched them nod.

"Yes," Dad said, slow and solemn. My mother touched her mouth with one hand and looked away.

"And Marica Brown is engaged to a soybean farmer?" I said.

"Yes," my dad answered. "I'm sorry."

I watched my parents nod.

"She couldn't wait, dear," my mom offered, her voice sad.

No shit? I thought. And then something of Marica came to me then. *You are going to carry me across the threshold?* I saw her say: her face back then, her staid gray stare and red hair in bangs. *You want me to cook your meals and darn your socks?*

But I only imitated my parents and nodded back at them, feeling this strange, wry smile on my lips. *Everything's a fucking waste,* I felt the urge to scream. *A fucking waste.*

I stood there a moment and looked at them. "I'm going to turn in," I said.

"Of course, dear," my mom said with a sad smile. My parents nodded at me.

"Of course," Dad echoed.

I managed to nod back

My dad rose with a big smile. He shook my hand and hugged me. "You can be proud of yourself, buster. You did your job," he told me. "You did what any good man would do."

I managed to nod for that, too, and I remembered to go and kiss my mother on the cheek.

"Sleep well, dear," Mom said.

"He hasn't said much," I heard her say as I left them with the TV. "That's not like him."

"He's tired," my dad said.

In my old room, I shut the door softly behind me without turning on the lights and stripped out of my uniform, letting it all fall to the floor. I found old high school sweats from memory in the chest of drawers, pulling them on in the faint

star light from the windows and the familiar, swaying silhouettes and shadows of the sweet gum trees outside. Falling
onto my old bed, I discovered the indent into the mattress
my teenage body had made was too small now and I realized
the hard knife handle was still in my sock. I lay there on my
back, in the quiet, listening to my breathing, feeling more
confident in the dark with the knife there against my ankle,
and thinking of humping it into the heat with my platoon
from the Hueys, their whirling blades over red dirt. I could
smell dried sweat, jasmine, perfume and then the streets and
the hot, humid air of Bin Hoa. The indent into the mattress
my teenage body had made was too small now. I focused on
the dead ceiling light above me, thinking the room was smaller, too, how time and place had become far away. I thought
how I had to remember to kiss my mother goodnight.

Later, I awoke with a start, recognizing from memory the
dark bedroom, its windows and then the quiet and steady
sound of my father's slow, paced steps as he went downstairs
into the basement to stoke and fill the furnace before bed.
I listened to his steps and remembered, too, how I used to
follow Dad's back in the twilight as a boy, placing my steps
behind his as we went outside to the barn in the evenings to
feed Mom's horses. I would walk in the cool fall and spring
or cold winter dusk behind his silhouette, through the quiet,
darkening and level pasture, alongside Mom's practice ring
and before the row of bare, dark pecan trees in the horizon,
the place where I learned how to ride a bicycle, how to shoot
a rifle; how to throw a curve and how to ride a horse. After
we fed, we would pause in the breeze way of the barn and
listen to the horses munch in their stalls, an occasional snort,
a stomp of a hoof, in the smell of sweet feed, dust, hair and

dried dung--and we would talk as a father and a son do, sometimes about nothing in particular; but what was more important, I realized, was that I felt his presence, I heard the communion in our voices. He was there for me.

I lay there and listened to my father's slow, steady steps go down to the furnace; I listened to them come back up. I saw him on the steps, saw his aged face, wandered in memory through the now still house I had grown up in, feeling as though I were a ghost walking through a shell with furniture, the wood floors and the frost green rooms; a ghost wondering where that boy was and where the likes of Foster was now; seeing Foster's cocky grin and look in the dining room wallpaper before Vietnam. I drifted to sleep, but jerked awake and sat up in my bed, swaying in the sudden drain of blood from my head, feeling the knife handle against my ankle and a slow spin of my old room in the night. An early sixties song came to me, for some reason, "On the Outside Looking in," and I rose, feeling the oak floor under my bare feet, listening to the house and a gentle wind outside and a lonesome, long-winding drone of an eighteen-wheeler on the highway.

In the pale light and shadows from the windows, I looked down at the dark, throw-down rug on the floor and at the other, made up, twin bed on the other side of the room, at the dim, tacked-on posters along the pale walls from the time before my first tour--an F-4 Phantom, Joe Namath about to throw a football in a New York Jets helmet and uniform, The Beatles looking on in long hair and costumes in *The Magical Mystery Tour* and Steppenwolf's *RIP Tombstone*. I did not need to see my dresser and mirror, the desk and bookshelves cluttered with high school books, magazines, comics, plane, car and rocket models; did not need to see my framed patches, artifacts and certificates along the wall from Airborne

School at Fort Bragg and Air Assault School at Fort Benning; and did not need to see that covering the inside of my bedroom door was the large and grim, light-on-dark poster from Airborne School: a skull clamping a bayonet in its cruel death grin, raining down from the sky against a backdrop of other skulls clamping bayonets, too, over the printed motto: *Death From Above.*

I knew from memory the simple, framed photos hung along the wall above my desk in the night of the room, and the more cluttered, unframed ones--wedged and likely curling now--that I could imagine, along the rim of my dresser mirror: younger, smiling Marica Browns, her red hair, her gray eyes, her smile and her white skin when she was my girlfriend; my tangerine orange SS Camaro, Foster Odom and his grinning, blonde girlfriend, Abbie Stewart; one or two photos with Foster Odom, Bubba Smith or Curtis Johnson, along with something of me in our hunting garb, baseball or football uniforms. I knew the smooth, youthful faces that knew nothing but God, country and Fermata Bend, Alabama, before our last prom and Vietnam. They smiled in longer hair and loud shirts, their smooth faces and curls or thin sideburns. They smiled, arm-in-arm or side-by-side, as if united together with their dates at that last prom. They stood on a makeshift, plyboard bridge lined in school-colored tissue paper and under a glittering, foil moon. I could feel that time without looking, feel it as lost and diaphanous; ideal and idyllic. *Blind faith,* I thought. Blind faith. Like a long and slow, Beatle love song.

A voice called me. *Beck-ie hon. Beck-ie.* I bolted up, sitting awake with a start, staring into gray light and a smiling, oval face. A nose, closed smile. Eyes too large. I watched the face speak a foreign name and scold, "Why aren't you covered up?" Its hand came forward and I sprang, grabbing its neck. The face went down, away, as I went up and over it, seemed to rise through gray mist and into the sudden frost green bedroom of my childhood: posters on the walls, dresser and mirror lined with photos, the cluttered desk and the bookshelves with the Hi-Fi stereo. Dawn light streamed through the windows and I was on the wood floor in old, tight high school sweats. My mother's neck was in my hand, her steel hair in a loose hair-wrap: her eyes bulging like a fish's, staring up at me from the floor, her mouth in an "O".

I released her, slowly stood up and stepped away.

"Don't ever do that," I said.

She sat up, gasping and staring at me, in an opened pink chamois bathrobe, white nightgown and slippers. "I thought ... I thought you...." she gasped, her voice hoarse, her eyes large on me, welling.

"Mom," I said. I went to help her up. She recoiled and brushed my hand away. She got to her feet and stepped back, her face stricken with terror.

"Mom," I tried.

She waved me off, backed away and out of the room, not blinking, not taking her look off me. I watched her go and discovered the opened switchblade from my ankle in my hand and felt the blood racing in my ears, suddenly aware that I was sweating, that my mouth was dry. The room seemed dead quiet, still and gray. I thought to follow her but spun around, seeing the gray Polaroid print in my mind of Foster's bloodied and mutilated head again--only this time grinning--impaled on a bamboo stick: a cruel, contrary and taunting grin. *You are going to die,* he said.

I knelt to the floor, pressed the point of the blade against the wood and up into the handle, until the blade clicked into place. I slid the switchblade handle into my waistband and in the arid and moth-balled closet of my hanging clothes, strewn boots, shoes and alongside my encased shotgun, I found a pair of old tennis shoes. I found athletic socks in the chest of drawers, sat on my bed, pulled them on over my first socks and then pulled on the shoes and tied the laces, standing up, nervous, scared, unable to stand still. I wanted a cigarette. I thought of the door, but turned and raised the bedroom window to the front yard, pushed out the screen and dropped outside to the ground.

In the shrubs, I knelt, gulped my thirst away at the water spigot; stood up, wiping my mouth on my sleeves, and began to run away from the house in the cold November air, over the frosted lawn and onto the chert drive, towards the county highway; feeling a suspension in the pounding of blood in my head and the steady rhythm of my feet, wanting to obliterate thought and memory and yearning for exhaustion before it began, the racing of my heart, the hard rasping of my breath. I turned up the county highway away from town, running alongside the graveled and dirt shoulder of the new blacktop, remembering to set a pace in the smell of the new tar and bright-painted lane lines, going by old rusted fence lines of pastures and pecan orchards, past weed-choked ditches, pine thickets and clay road turnoffs before trashed yards and poor blacks' shacks. Off the road looked the same as what I had come from, grown up in, only it didn't feel the same. I lifted my feet and held my head up the way I had been taught in high school track, the way I used to run with Foster and Curtis in the springs and summers to get in shape. I was in shape now, but different, I was hard and lean; I was taut and tense.

I held my pace and didn't stop. The sunlight grew. An occasional, winding eighteen-wheeler bore down and blasted by me. My feet grew heavy, my mouth began to wag open with my breathing, my heart pounded. And I kept going, holding the pace, wanting to hurt, wanting the limit of my endurance, one step after the other--until everything blurred and my whole being seemed to become a stumbling, symphonic roaring of feet, heart and lungs and my legs would no longer behave. I was still moving, unaware of, nor caring of the speed or of where I was, face down, aching for air, when the ground rushed up at me. I rolled through thick weeds and sage, stopping with whirling spots before my eyes, my heart and lungs coursing, my throat raw. I made myself get up, turn and stagger out of the ditch and into woods with my head down, my hands on my hips, trying to find breath and eventually recognizing the logging trail I was on, overgrown in briars and dead scuppernong vines. I thought of a trip wire or a pangee trap. But they would not be here.

I walked down the trail, into the thick stillness of the woods, regaining my breath, feeling a relief in the exhaustion, feeling tired and purged, and recognizing the smell of decaying leaves and the damp earth in the cool fall air. Somewhere along here, Jared Snead had run his hounds and Marica Brown and I had ridden horseback. Foster and I had nailed a fox's skull to a poplar tree on a deer blind we had built out of tarp and two by fours. Something of Marica came to me then. I saw her in jeans, sitting her horse; red pigtails, grey eyes and a smile. I saw Jared make his short, high laugh in his worn hunting garb. I heard the *plinking* of General Beauregard's piano keys.

A twig snapped, and without thought, I hit the ground on my stomach, my heart racing, and my eyes and ears alert. A steady plodding and crunching of footsteps came from the other side of a creek. I relaxed then, feeling silly, lying in the dead leaves and briars below the rise of an oak trunk. A man and two boys appeared in hunting coats, hunting boots and florescent orange caps, each cradling a rifle in the crock of his arm with the muzzle pointing up. I recognized Coach Watson, my junior high football coach. He was short and more heavy-set now; the same long nose, darting eyes and the same short, black moustache.

I watched as they stopped, unloaded their rifles, held them over their heads and stepped across the creek; the boys imitating Coach Watson and his steps, following him single-file. They passed by me on the trail as I lay stock still. I thought of how easily they could be jumped. I could grab coach from behind. *Boo, coach!* I could say. I could knock him down, the man who ran me to death so I could be a member of the team, who preached teamwork and quoted the Bible and generals Patton, Grant and Lee and talked about how to be a good citizen and a man, who wanted his players to be tough and to believe in themselves and do as they were told.

As their boot steps faded away, I then thought to jump up and call coach's name, go forward and introduce myself. I could see Coach Watson and the boys stop, turn around; Coach Watson pause, grin and exclaim *Ha!* as he did in practice or before the campfire during hunts. I could see his face announce: *Boys, boys. This here is Beck Senecal,* he would turn to them and make me an example.

Class of Sixty-Eight, Coach would declare. *One of the best damn linebackers you ever saw, along with* ... but then he couldn't say it, with a brief, sad smile and a hesitant, emphatic nod. *This here is one of the best of us,* Coach would cover himself. *He did his duty for his country.* He would pause. *And now he's come back home.*

I could envision my old coach stepping forward, grinning at me with mutual respect now, shaking my hand and maybe slapping me on the shoulder. I could see myself as worthy now in his eyes, as we boys in Fermata Bend always sought to be worthy. The young boys with Coach Watson would look up at me with small and wondering grins, cradling their rifles. And I could just nod and not say anything, knowing their imaginations would take over.

Running back toward Fermata Bend, along the shoulder of new blacktop, I breathed through clenched teeth against the pain shooting up my legs on every step, and held a pace, facing the oncoming traffic. I welcomed the hurt, wanting to extract a price for being alive, imagining the soles of my feet bleeding into my socks and into my flimsy, thin tennis shoes. Passing drivers waved to me in that small-town, southern mannerism I had grown up in. I didn't recognize anyone, I wondered if anyone recognized me. But out of old habit, I waved back, in semblance of memory, how Foster, Curtis and I used to wave, too, running along the older, rougher road together to get in shape, back when each of us had a belief in winning.

Suddenly I missed them and wanted to belong again. How did we get so separated? I felt a wrenching urge to turn and run into the woods, to be swallowed whole; a wish to disappear forever into the very trees, the river and the river roads, the time and place that we knew and had grown up in, a wish to be swallowed by this land until I could be swallowed and buried no further; somewhere deep, private and never to be found again; and where--I imagined myself like an old Creek Indian beginning to utter his Death Chant--I might close my eyes, kneel and place my head to the ground, onto the only thing that lasts, and weep for everything that does not.

But I didn't. I gritted my teeth and waved at the periodic, passing drivers. I kept placing one foot in front of the other; my throbbing feet growing numb, my head beginning to spin in the roar of my breathing, spots dancing before my eyes.

A throbbing beat of rock music came out of nowhere, a hard squeal of tires. The light green body of a Pontiac GTO on the blacktop drew up close, alongside me, and I looked up, startled and breathless, into a strawberry blonde girl's smiling face in wide, mirrored sunglasses, behind the wheel. The car's windows were down; its T-tops were off. The rolling, mild, fall sky reflected off the car's windshield.

"What's happening, baby?" the girl quipped above the music. "You trying out for the team again?"

The GTO squealed ahead of me, pullied off the road and braked hard. I stumbled to a stop, panting and staring at the solid-colored car with blending plastic bumpers and no chrome. The engine and the music cut off together. The driver's door opened and the girl stepped out slowly from the car in knit brown slacks, brown dress boots and a brown corduroy jacket lined in white fleece. Her mirrored sunglasses glinted soft sunlight. Her blonde hair was colored and short now. Her flared nose was the same. It was Abbie, Abbie Stewart. Foster's girl. I bowed my head and planting my hands on my knees. My feet burned. I couldn't breathe fast enough.

"I thought to run over you," Abbie dead-panned. "Be *so* glad I didn't."

I closed my eyes and wagged my head at her. I opened my eyes as she came toward me in dancing spots, like a pulsating mirage. She stopped and the vision of her steadied. The mirrored sunglasses covered too much of her face, I thought. Her mouth closed into a small line of umber-colored lips. I bowed my head, wanting breath.

"Well, now," Abbie said, her tone false and bright, "aren't we looking good?"

I tried to laugh but couldn't. When I did manage to look up, Abbie's mouth had pursed into a frown and her hands were pushed deep into her coat pockets.

"No," she corrected herself with a shake of her head, hair, her tone sober. "Take that back. You don't look so good."

It seemed funny, bizarre. I managed something of a guffaw and straightened up, feeling the blood drain from my head. A pickup truck honked and passed us. We both turned and waved.

"Marica told me you were back," Abbie said. "She also told me about Dea."

"So, Marica's talking to you?" I said.

"At least Marica's talking to me."

I grinned and shook my head. A farmer's flatbed truck honked and passed by us. We both turned and waved.

"Take off those sunglasses," I said.

Abbie hesitated. She slowly pulled a hand from her coat pocket and lifted the mirrored sunglasses up and set them onto her hair, letting her hand drop. I saw she had on light brown eye shadow, dark eye liner and mascara. Her small blue eyes shifted and wouldn't meet mine.

"Never thought I'd see you like that," I said.

"Like what?" Abbie whined.

"You're dressed up, made up," I said. "I don't know...

grown up, I guess." I shook my head and looked away at the distant treetops and the quiet fields.

"And what am I supposed to look like?" Abbie said, her tone morose. "You thought everything would stay the same? Everything's changed, Beck," Abbie sighed. "Foster's dead. And so are others. And you...you broke Marica's heart."

I felt The Disconnect then, coming over me. I turned to her. Abbie's hand was back in the coat pocket and she was frowning. I tried to hold my bitter laugh in, seeing her smooth, thin face with light blush, her shorter hair now, her small blue eyes. I wanted a cigarette bad. I thought of Foster then and how we now seemed like such naïve, gung ho kids.

"And you?" I said. "Did you change, too?"

"I just wanted someone," Abbie said, her voice going hard. Her look became steady, her face sad. "And I lost him."

I nodded. My feet burned.

"After Foster's body came home, I dropped out of Auburn," Abbie informed me, "and I came back to Fermata Bend to try to be happy...because, well, I thought there wasn't anyplace else to go," she sighed. "Fermata Bend has always been me. But the truth is, Becky-boy--Fermata Bend is becoming a place you can't go back to. If I don't go back to Auburn," she added, "I'll be going somewhere."

She paused, as though I should say something. But I couldn't think of what to say. Instead, I watched as she ran a quick hand through the back of her hair and shoved it into the pocket of her jacket.

"I've been working in Daddy's hardware and going to every concert I can," Abbie said, looking away down the highway and then back to me. "John Denver. Gordon Light- foot," she said. "The Tams, anywhere and anyone I want to drive to." She made a sad smile. "It lets me pretend, lets me not think while I'm waiting for my life to go on."

I remembered Dea then. I still didn't know what to say. Abbie's hand came back out of the pocket and she lowered the mirrored sunglasses over her eyes. I watched her small mouth, tried to see past the glasses, my feet feeling as if they were bare and on hot pavement. I began lifting one foot and then the other.

"Well, good luck," I said. "Who's Marica's lucky husband-to-be?"

"Oh," she said. "Don't you know?"

I lied, shaking my head no.

"Roddy," Abbie informed me, matter-of-fact. "Roddy Sexton. He has long blonde hair and granny glasses? He runs his daddy's farm. And he *loves* her," Abbie let me know.

"Did he change, too?"

"No, I guess not," Abbie answered with a small shake of her head, her tone matching my sarcasm. "He tried that male, bravado thing with the rest of you--but he flunked his physical with a curvature spine. Tsk. Tsk," she nodded. "Lucky Marica," she said.

"I know you boys aren't queer," Abbie said, her voice growing bitter. "But y'all sure act alike--doing what you think the old men want you to do. Still," she added, with a confident nod, "Foster would not have done what you did to Marica."

"Don't be so sure," I said, feeling anger rising in me and giving her as mean a grin as I could, watching her sunglassed face, hopping from one foot to the other. "I daresay I knew him better than you did. He would have done the same damn thing, sweetheart."

Abbie shook her head. "No, you're wrong," she insisted. "You're wrong. He loved me," she said. "He *loved* me." "He was one of us, too, baby," I said. "And don't you forget it."

A horn sounded. I turned and waved at a passing pickup truck. But Abbie didn't. She stood there, her mirrored sunglasses on me, not saying anything. I wondered if she was staring at me or looking away.

"Don't you tell me he didn't love me," Abbie insisted, in almost a hiss. Her mouth pinched small. "Don't you dare tell me that."

"I won't tell you that, Abbie," I said. I shook my head no. I watched her and hopped from one foot to the other. "But he did what he was told.

"And I'll tell you this," I said. "He wanted to be worthy, too. Like all of us." I watched her and kept hopping from one foot to the other. "We all wanted to be worthy," I admitted.

"*Worthy*," Abbie echoed, in her same, almost hiss. "Worthy," she sneered.

"Well, I'll tell you *this,* Beck Senecal," Abbie's voice rose at me. "There aren't going to be any more Foster Odoms." She nodded in hard emphasis. "There aren't going to be any more boys who believe in their fathers." She nodded. "This war has seen to that. This war that goes nowhere, does nothing and never ends. This war has done that."

She bit her lip and turned away. I didn't say anything, watching her back as I hopped from one foot to the other.

"I'm sorry Abbie," I called after a moment, staring at her back and hopping. She didn't answer.

"I'm sorry. Marica could have waited," I said.

"Not forever," Abbie answered with her back to me. She shook her head and hair. "Not anymore, Becky-boy," she said, turning to me. "We don't have to be the old women anymore, either. We don't have to be," she paused, "your obedient servants."

At that, she angered me. I felt like I didn't matter. I watched Abbie's face, the sunglasses and her moving lips, forming words I didn't hear and feeling the slow and hard Disconnect. I saw myself killing her, slowly stepping forward and slicing her throat from the front, from ear to ear, while she kept talking, her head and sunglasses toppling over, revealing a stubbed neck fountain of pulsing blood, while her body would still stand and her mouth would keep talking from the head on the ground. *Foster's girlfriend.* I pulled back the thought, felt ashamed.

"--Why?" she wanted to know, her voice plaintive and sad. "*Why* is it in Fermata Bend men have to do what men do?" She paused and stood there, waiting, as though I had the answer. Her mouth slightly opened. Her mirrored sunglasses glinted.

"Why did he have to die?" she said. "Why couldn't he have just loved me?"

I shook my head to rid the previous thought, to try and hear her. I hopped from one foot to the other. I shook my head. I didn't have an answer.

"It was supposed to be simple, Beck," Abbie went on, her voice sad. "Back then, I just wanted to be married. Maybe go to the junior college...I just wanted to have babies like my momma did, make the beds and wash his underwear...I just wanted to know he was there for me, minding his family farm...but then...but then...." she stuttered, paused and sighed. She drew a hand out of her pocket and doffed it, palm open, to the sky. "Y'all had to *volunteer*," she said, her tone exasperated. "Jesus," she said. "Fucking volunteer," she said. "The Fermata Bend tradition.

"Things will never be simple again," she declared. Abbie lifted her sunglasses and dabbed her eyes on her sleeves. She lowered her glasses, paused and turned away. I couldn't think of anything to say. Hopping from one foot to the other, I watched her walk to the green GTO.

Even if you're right, I thought in defiance of her, *I can live with myself. I can be proud. I can walk downtown and look everyone in the face, sister. Even if you're right.*

Abbie stopped at the GTO's driver's door and turned back to me with a shake of her head, her sunglasses. I made myself grin at her and I kept hopping from one foot to the other. She made a closed, sad smile, got into the driver's side of the car and slammed the door closed. The engine started, the headers boomed, the sound system blared on in fast, loud rock. I still held my grin, hopping from one foot to the other, while the GTO took off with a short, squealing catch of the tires on the new blacktop.

I stopped hopping then, enduring the burning in my feet, waiting to catch my breath. I fingered under the waistband of my sweats and found the bulge of Vin Trough's switchblade pressing into my waist. I slipped the handle out, palmed it, and after looking at it for a long moment, I threw it as hard as I could over a barbed wire fence beyond a ditch, into a field.

My mother took a step back as I came into the kitchen in my soiled, wet sweats and blood-soaked tennis shoes. "Steve," she uttered, her eyes went over me, her look afraid. I tried to grin for her, not like I had for Abbie. But she backed further away, staring, cross-palming her elbows to the waist of her house dress.

"I-I won't hurt you," I said, shaking my head no. "I won't hurt you, Mom. I-I threw the knife away," I offered, grinning. I held up my dirtied palms to her. My hands trembled in fatigue.

She stared at me. "How can you go to church tomorrow?" she blurted. Her lower lip trembled. "How can everyone see you?"

I looked at her. I didn't have an answer.

Later, I cried against the searing pain of my raw blisters in the hot water of the shower, hardly able to stand it. But I managed another grin at my mother afterwards, sitting in the lounge chair of the family room before the dead TV, in an old pair of denim cut-offs and a t-shirt as she doctored and bandaged my feet on the ottoman, silent and shooting me quick, worried glances.

My father came home in his suit and tie from the insurance office. "Son," he beamed. "There you are."

Mother motioned to him. He looked at me, looked at her, followed her into the kitchen and then they came out later into the family room where I sat there with my bandaged feet up. Dad seated himself beside me on the lounge chair's armrest, with his mouth closed and a solemn gaze, while my mother looked on from the doorway, her mouth small and closed.

"It's Foster, isn't it?" Dad said. He nodded when I did.

"All of them," I whispered. "How do you live with it?"

I watched his face fall, watched his lips purse into a thin line. Dad bowed his head.

"It's happened to all of us," he said. "It's happened to all of us."

Dad nodded to Mom. She covered her mouth with her hands. Her eyes welled. She turned away and left.

"You've, er," Dad took a deep breath, "got your mom," he lowered his voice, "a little worried." He gave me a knowing look. "You know," he said.

I nodded, watching his middle-aged, weathered and expectant face, trying to imagine if his transformation could have been the same as mine, trying to imagine if he had lived long enough to forget, or at least, to forget himself. He had come home to the tradition of his father, and his father; that there was a purpose, that America was Right, that a job was done. He had come home to a parade and a girl. He had come back to a time of Fermata Bend where he could pick up where he had left off, go back, in some way, to what he was. I looked at his aging face, remembering he had been at

the Battle of the Bulge. At Saint Vith, there was a road in
the freezing snow. They leveled the howitzers and stopped
the German armored advance on the other side. The line was
clear. Us and them. Right or wrong. Do or die.

But all I had was heat, ambushes and positions we dubbed
"Point Endless," positions we humped toward through jungle,
following a reconnaissance patrol's report, against invisible
snipers and booby traps; positions of poor, farming Vietnamese, thatched huts and rice paddies; positions we secured, only
to find little or nothing, then leave and come back to again.
The enemy was indistinctive, elusive. Who was he? Nothing
changed. There was never an end in sight.

"It's hard," Dad said, glancing to the doorway. "You never
forget," he whispered. He slid his hands in and out of his
pants pockets, folded them in his lap.

"Everything will come around, Beck," Dad squeezed his
eyes shut. "Trust me. You did your job. You've just got to
take it easy, take your time." He opened his eyes. "You will
learn to leave it behind and come home."

"Leave it behind," I echoed, watching him. "Home."

Dad nodded. "Takes some time," he said. "And work.
Hey, you need to get to work...." His voice brightened, he
changed the subject. "How about you take your time and do
some work for me?"

"Work?" I echoed the word, watching his face.

"Yeah, get to work," he said. "Work is what you need.
The pecan orchards," he suggested, nodding. "I need somebody to take the field truck through the rows this winter. You
know," he said, "like you and--."

He caught himself, paused. "Well, like y'all used to do,"
Dad corrected himself. "You know. Prune, cut and patch,"
he said. "I need you to inspect all the rows for me." Dad
smiled, nodded.

I imitated his smile, his nod, remembering how Foster and I used to work the pecan orchards as teenagers. I thought of being alone out there this time, being outside with the physical work.

"You can do it on your own time," Dad said. "What do you say? And of course, I'll pay you."

"Yeah," I nodded. "Yeah, work. Maybe I need to work," I said.

Dad slapped my shoulder. "Hey, no hurry. It's November," he said. "It'll be ready when you are." He smiled. "But you rest now. You just take it easy. And we'll talk, okay?" He nodded, squeezed my shoulder. "We'll talk," he promised.

I nodded and Dad smiled. But somehow it all seemed sad. It seemed like we were mis-communicating, talking in different languages, that he couldn't come from where I was.

He squeezed my shoulder and rose and left for the office. Mother brought me a glass of orange juice. I held the glass while she left. She came back with some wool socks and a pair of worn chukkas. Mom knelt and gently pulled them over my bandaged feet.

"There," she fussed over me, trying for her old voice, her old tone. "There," she braved a smile at me as she rose. I nodded, holding the juice. She waited until I thought to drink it, took the glass and left. She came back with a bowl of cream of wheat. She stood by as I ate.

"Thank you, Mom," I remembered to say.

And I remembered to smile and thank her before I limped back into my still bedroom with its dusty, plastic kit models, magazines, adolescent posters on the walls and small, curling photographs of images and people I once knew, stuck along the edges of the dressing mirror. In the quiet of my old bedroom, I shut and locked the door, feeling alone and safe before I lay down to sleep, tired and aching as I wanted to be, too tired to think, or to remember, or to dream.

In the morning, I begged out of church, sitting at the breakfast table in old flannel pajamas, peeling off my bloody foot bandages. "I can't do it, Mom," I said. "I'm sorry." I looked her in the face and gave her what I hoped was a wistful frown. Across the table, my mother pressed her lips together into a thin line of disappointment. She looked to my dad. Dad didn't look up, didn't say anything, but mouthed his eggs over his plate, in his clean shirt and tie. Mother made a thin smile over her plate at me. She was in fresh red lipstick, rouge, and in a new black and tan dress with matching pumps. She had washed and combed her short hair and set in a middle hairpiece. She had ironed my khaki uniform, too, early that morning while I slept. It hung stiff and straight off hangers on the doorway sill of the bathroom. She had prepared my old favorite breakfast of grits, sausage and eggs.

"Oh, Beck. I wanted everyone to see you," she sighed. "I wanted to show them how proud of you we are."

"I will--later," I said and nodded. "Promise. Next week."

Mother started to speak, but Dad cleared his throat. She stopped and waited for him.

"Well, let's go, then, Mel," he said, taking a last swig of coffee.

Mother looked at me with that thin, closed smile. She sighed and rose from the table with Dad.

"All right," Dad stated. "You going to be okay here?"

"Yeah," I nodded. "I'll be okay."

"We'll going to be gone most of the day," Mom reminded me. "Driving around and visiting everyone. You know."

I nodded. That was what people did on Sundays in Fermata Bend.

"All right, then," Dad stated. He took up his dark suit coat off the back of his chair while mother held a thin smile on me. She came around the table and gave me a quick kiss on the cheek. My father looked to her as he pulled on his coat. He nodded to me. They both hesitated, turned away.

I sat at the kitchen table and listened to their soft, fading steps; a murmur, a pause.

"Oh, and Beck," my dad called.

"Yes, sir?" I answered.

"There's a letter sitting on the table here for you." A pause. "From a Dea Banes at Pecan Real Estate."

"Oh, okay," I called.

"Who is that?" I heard my mother murmur.

I heard their footsteps, the opening and closing of the front door, and then felt the ensuing silence of the house. I rose from the table and limped into the living room, letting myself fall across the couch, peering out the double front windows, past the yard and the sweet gum trees. I listened. I heard car doors shut. I heard the car crank, idle and back out. I watched my parents' maroon Oldsmobile 88 drive away, the tires crunching down the chert drive, through the field. The car grew small, trailing dust to the highway. It turned and was gone. On the coffee table, I saw the long, lone business envelope, the handwriting in dark blue ink. I picked it up and let it drop.

I rose from the couch, waited, wanting to be sure they did not turn back, feeling the stillness, the quiet and the weight of the house; remembering what church used to be like: Reverend Hirsch's balding head, his bespeckled face and closed smile, a demeanor too sweet, too kind, too full of belief; I remembered smiling people and the opening of doors: Dad parking under the cedar trees before the yard of the gray, antebellum church; me getting out again and again in my Sunday suits, cleaned shoes, my scrubbed face and combed hair, opening the back car door for Mom; smiling for everyone and glancing around for Foster or Marica. Dad and I followed Mom, opening the doors of the church for her, following her down the carpeted aisle to our family pew (in the middle, on the left). Mom led us in, smiling and nodding for everyone. I felt Fermata Bend's eyes on me, my dad behind me. We filed into the pew. We sat when mother sat. We sat through the service, sang the hymns like "Onward Christian Soldier," "Amazing Grace," or "All Things Bright and Beautiful." We sat through the stern, admonishing or sweet sermons of Reverend Hirsch and Jared Snead, bare headed and in some worn, double-breasted jacket, voicing his loud "Amens" at the end of every prayer. We followed Mom's cues on the hymns and the prayers and the offering, among the confident voices of belief and obedience, the voices of belonging, like much of Fermata Bend, Alabama.

We rose when Mom rose. We followed her to the communion rail and back. We followed her outside when the service was over, past the ever-smiling minister at the door, to the smiling and talking friends and neighbors in the church

yard: the quiet, bare-headed and grinning Jared Snead in an
old, clean coat, the other veterans of my childhood in suits
and with their wives in pretty dresses, their sons and their
daughters all in Sunday clothes, too; we smiled and talked
to the same smiling and talking people we knew, our church
segregated by race and habit and the ingrained association of
old families.

Then Dad and I followed Mom to the car under the
cedars, where I opened and closed the rear passenger door
for her; my father got in behind the wheel and I got into the
front passenger's seat, shutting the door. At Louie's Restaurant on the town square, I got out and opened and closed
the car door for Mom when Dad parked at the curb, and I
opened the restaurant door as Mom led us in. I pulled her
table chair and she sat before we did, smiling for her family
men, smiling for anyone, chatting and taking her time with
the menu while the waitress brought sweet tea and rolls. I
imagined eyes were on us then, too, while mother and I told
dad what we wanted and dad ordered. I felt Fermata Bend's
eyes on us then, too, while we ate and spoke to others. After
the meal, I pulled mother's chair for her while we left, smiling and nodding again. I opened the restaurant door, the car
door for her, and all Sunday afternoon, I smiled and opened
car and house doors while we drove and visited distant family,
friends and neighbors.

Sundays, we dressed. Sundays, we smiled. Sundays, we
visited. Sundays, I was always taught, there were eyes on me.

I turned away from the couch and the window and
limped into the bathroom, past the stiff, still uniform hanging
from the doorjamb that Mom had ironed for me. I brushed
my teeth and carefully shaved, noting again the gaunt, hol-
lowed eyes on my thin face in the lavatory mirror. Under the

sink, I found a bottle of peroxide. Sitting on the closed toilet lid, I propped my feet over the rim of the bathtub, gritted my teeth and emptied the bottle on my feet. I found a towel and dried my feet off. Limping into my old bedroom, I dropped my pajamas in the closet, pulled jeans on over my briefs and pulled an old hunting shirt over my tee shirt. I sat on the unmade bed and re-bandaged my feet. I put on two pair of clean athletic socks from the drawers and slipped my feet into the worn chukkas that mother had found for me yesterday. I took an old hunting jacket out of the closet and I hobbled out of the room.

The car was still there, mounted on the cinder blocks in the shed below the house, under the now dusty canvas cover beside my mother's baby blue, double-wide horse trailer. In the crossed morning light that streamed into the arid air and floating motes from the opened doorway behind me and the shed's side window pane over my Dad's long work table, the dust-coated, custom egg butt wheels and tires could be seen beneath the canvas rim. Above the car, in the roof, was the old family canoe, lying parallel and upside down on the padded rafters, among broken dirt dobber nests, cob webs and dust-coated camping equipment hung from high pegs along the walls.

I turned back the canvas to the bright orange hood, its loud white lines; the chrome hood emblem and the shiny black radiator grill. My hot rod Camaro seemed like a bright, lost toy from another time, and if I had died in Vietnam, I pondered, whatever it had meant to me or to memory would have been lost forever.

I thought of the car sitting until the end of my parents'
time, or until it became like old cars on farms do, rusted
and sitting, or maybe winding up in some collector's garage
or in some other gleeful kid's hands. I realized all memories
associated with things had been lost by Foster Odom and
they are lost by everyone in time. I recalled I had longer hair
before Vietnam and I believed in the magic and the music
from the DJs on the radio. I believed in the men's approval
through sports and hunting. Marica Brown was mysterious
and unique. I could remember her riding horseback, smiling
and singing "My Green Tambourine." I believed we were
special. I believed her steady, slate gray eyes held me and saw
nothing else. Her long, red hair. Her firm, pale torso. Her
quick laugh. We initiated first sex on the orange hood of the
Camaro, pressing against each other under pine trees somewhere, in a breeze, on a night with the car radio on. I lost
myself in her and when I came to, I saw Marica seeing me, a
steady gaze, a slow, tentative smile; her long, sweaty hair slung
to one side of her face, our sweaty bodies sticking to the hood
while we lay apart. When she sighed, I believed in the moment. I believed in The Young Rascals then, The Beach Boys
and Herman's Hermits, while each began and ended a song
for us on the car radio.

You come back now, I remembered her mouth and words
the last time I saw her at the train station. She looked at me.
You come back now.

I rolled the canvas up and off the car and set it on Dad's
work table. I found the spare keys in the rusty coffee can on
the shelf beside the window. In the Camaro's trunk, everything was there, preserved as if in a vacuum: the tool box and
the H-jack, unopened cans of oil, an oil filter, a can of brake
fluid, spare belts and hoses, and a can of spray lubricant. I re-

discovered the shriveled brown plug of a corsage, Marica's silk leg garter from the senior prom and two used, dried Trojans in a wadded-up paper bag.

I lifted the tool box out, leaving the trunk opened. I found a tire gauge in the tool box, turned on my father's electric air compressor in the corner and unraveled the compressor hose as I went around the car and re-inflated the tires. Turning off the compressor and re-wrapping the hose, I ignored the steady throbbing in my feet, crawled under the car with the tool box and bled the brakes, letting the fluid run into an old metal bucket that was already there. I drained the oil pan into the bucket, unscrewed the oil filter and dropped it into the bucket, too. I tightened the brake lines, came out from under the car, lined the seal of the new oil filter at the trunk with old oil off my fingers, crawled back under the car and screwed on the new oil filter. I pulled the bucket out from under the car, took the H-jack out of the trunk and slowly jacked up the front of the car, tugging out the front cinder blocks and then lowering the car onto its front wheels. I jacked up the rear of the car and did the same.

My feet throbbed and I ignored them. The rest was easy and I took my time. My parents were gone and I could relax. And if they found me out, well then, I'd tell them the truth. Alone with the car after two years, in the still, arid air of the shed, in the growing daylight from the window and the opened doorway, I lit cigarettes on my Zippo and smoked while I worked, trying not to think too much, or to remember, or to pretend to relish what I was doing, only working on the car as something that was once habit and familiar. I opened and lifted the hood, checked the distributor, the rotor and the points. I gapped and replaced the spark plugs, using the old gaper and socket and wrench set from the tool box. I removed the air filter unit, checked the floats in the Holley four-barreled carburetor, examined the air filter, the hoses and the belts, remembering how Foster and I, talking and joking, as boys will do, drained the gas tank with a vacuum hose and jacked the car up together onto the cinder blocks. We took out the battery and filled the radiator with ethanol. We sprayed lubricant into the carburetor and onto the hoses and the belts.

Without Foster now, I drained the ethanol from the radiator into another old, metal bucket. I tightened the drain plug, poured radiator fluid and then water from the outside hose into the radiator. I capped my dad's pressure gauge onto the radiator neck, pumped up the gauge and checked the water pump and the hoses for leaks. I removed the gauge, topped the radiator off with water and replaced the radiator cap. I poured new brake fluid into the hydraulic reservoir, topping it off at the "full" line. I punched open the oil cans with a screwdriver on my dad's work shelf and poured the new oil through a funnel from the tool box into the crankcase. I capped the crankcase and checked the oil level on the oil stick. Outside the shed, I made three trips with two gallon gas cans from my father's gasoline pump at the tractor shed, pouring the gasoline into the Camaro's tank and replacing the cap. With a screwdriver from the tool box, I removed the battery from my father's International pickup truck in the driveway and carried it down to the shed, gritting my teeth against the pain of my feet in their chukkas on the chert. I set the battery into the Camaro's metal battery tray, tightening the battery side clamps and hooking up the cables.

Before I tried to start the car, I cleaned up my mess, turned away, paused, and lit another cigarette on my Zippo, smoking and gazing out the doorway at the early afternoon field and the highway beyond, feeling a pulsating burn in my feet, thinking how I was not hungry and then suddenly thinking of my platoon humping it toward a dust-off somewhere in the heat of Vietnam.

I dropped the cigarette and stepped on it, turned to the car and leaned over the engine, under the opened hood. I picked up the gas can and poured a little gas into the carburetor. I set the can down off in the corner, disconnected the rotor cap from the rotor with a screwdriver, hobbled to the driver's door, opened it and slid into the black bucket seat behind the steering wheel. I pushed in the clutch, pumped the accelerator, turned the key in the ignition two, three times. The engine turned. I got out of the car, limped to the engine, poured more gas into the carburetor, set the can away and set the rotor cap on. Back behind the wheel, I pushed in the clutch, pumped the accelerator and turned the ignition. The engine whinnied, turned and died. I cranked it again. The engine coughed and then boomed to life, roaring, idling fast and hard, filling up the shed in noise, exhaust and dust. I thought of Foster then, closed my eyes for him, grinned and coughed. I let the engine run, the noise deafening, the headers filling and droning, the way I remembered. I opened my eyes, got out, replaced the air filter and air filter unit over the carburetor and closed the hood, the trunk, got back in behind the wheel and shut the door. I grinned and tested the brakes and the clutch on my tender feet.

When the engine's idling settled, I put the car into gear, let my foot off the clutch and eased the car out of the shed and into the daylight. It felt lonely, like coming out of a tomb, a long sleep; the car awakened, angry, defiant, throaty and alive, after all, its headers droning. I made myself listen to the engine and check the gauges on the dash, and I remembered to buckle myself in. I let the clutch out and the car surged, rumbling and roaring down the path and up onto the drive from the house, the tires spinning up chert and dust. I had forgotten the feel of speed and power. I braked hard at the white fence and the mailbox, despite the pain in my feet, downshifting, letting out the clutch and turning the Camaro onto the highway, toward Fermata Bend.

The engine pitched and roared on each gear, the car sped and seemed to rise into a hum in the bright, cool afternoon. I pulled the car into the passing lane and shot past Dea in her white convertible Lincoln with the real estate signs on the doors and the top down, waving to her as she turned her blonde Afro head to look, the wind slanting her Afro, her mouth opened in surprise. She was in something like an orange cardigan with a white scarf on her neck. Beside her in the front passenger's seat was a middle-aged, bald, black man in a dark Sunday suit. In the back seat, in their Sunday clothes, too, was a white woman seated with two identical beige-skinned girls in kinky pigtails. I looked back. I had never seen that in Fermata Bend.

I pushed the accelerator to the floor. The car roared and rose. The landscape on either side of me blurred. I shot past an old white couple in a Dodge sedan, then past a rusty, GMC pickup truck, and turned back into my lane before an oncoming eighteen wheeler, letting off the gas. The blast and suck of the wind. I grinned in the re-acquainted thrill and giddiness of it, the speed and the motions, the surging and the winding of the engine, and remembering, too, how the real joy was when there was no destination.

Alone in my home town on a quiet Sunday, for the first time since Vietnam, I lit a cigarette on my Zippo, downshift-

ed and turned the Camaro off Main Street at the second light
before the town square and drove down the long and quiet
Verbena Street, its framed houses, well-kept lawns, sidewalks
and old hardwood trees, sensing the absence of people and the
slow decadence of time around me, the smell of damp earth
and dead leaves. I turned down Butter and Egg Street toward
Marica's green house, its large, even yard and the two familiar
cars in the garage: the yellow Barracuda and the green LTD.
I downshifted and slowed the Camaro to a roll, recalling my
anticipation when I used to pull in to be welcomed inside,
and thinking how, if she was in the house now, she could not
miss hearing and remembering the sound of my hot rod.

　　Nothing moved. I cruised slowly by, watching the house,
the car's headers droning. They were likely out of church, just
out of the town diner. Maybe they were visiting a neighbor,
or a neighbor was visiting them. Then one of front window
blinds flashed and rose and I saw Marcia's face behind the
window pane, peering out with a slight, quizzical look. And
her eyes met mine. She paused and then she lowered the
blinds back down. I braked the car to a stop and looked
back at the house, feeling the engine idle. A long moment
and nothing moved. I couldn't make myself go to the door.
I thought of her family, their faces, and worse, I thought of
Roddy Sexton.

　　I let the car roll on, turned down the next street, suddenly feeling those Saturday nights at the Cherokee Drive-In,
remembering Marica's long, red hair and how she used to look
at me; seeing her laugh, her smile, and recalling how I used to
hold her in the car or on her parents' sofa.

　　You are going to carry me across the threshold? she said. *You
want me to cook your meals and darn your socks?*

I grinned at that and then remembered how I grinned, too, when I slit a wounded and wheezing VC's throat under a canopy of trees and pristine star light, as he lay wheezing for breath on a trail after our platoon carried out a night ambush near Binh Thai. *For Foster,* I grinned at him. *Tai Sao? Tai Sao?* I suddenly saw Vin Trough crying, and felt The Disconnect. Her spilled hair, her small, desperate look in loud make up. *We're just temporary,* I had said, grinning at her, too. *We're just temporary.*

Out of town and roaring north in the Camaro on the vacant highway, I felt the wind and the car's old power under me. *Good weather for Chevies,* I remembered from somewhere. *The only rod's an American rod,* I heard Foster. His boast. His eager, blonde face. The grin before Vietnam. About four miles out of town, past Tillman's wood frame Country Store and gas station, I turned off onto the familiar, dry, dirt road, among the thick trees, toward the river and I turned on the radio to WLS, like I used to do. "The Night They Drove Old Dixie Down," by Joan Baez, came on; then bright, peppy commercials for Rolaids, Nehi Soda and Marlborough Reds. Then another unfamiliar song, called "Uncle Albert," came on, by Paul and Linda McCartney. I let the car coast, dust pluming behind me while the long song went on and on, changing tempos. It sounded odd, it seemed strange. It was Paul McCartney with his wife, not The Beatles. I listened beyond the radio to the droning and rolling of the engine against the quiet of the woods and fields. I slowed at the Odom's house, braking before the swing gate of the white post fence and the rusted, metal mailbox topped in dead scuppernong vines.

The front yard was still in pine trees, blanketed in pine needles. The blue frame house was still weathered with its grey mansard roof and dull white, Tudor-arched railing on the wrap-around porch. I cut the radio and the motor. I set the parking brake and I sat a moment in the car, in the awkward and sudden stillness, remembering I had parked here before; and then I realized the dogs were gone.

In the side yard of the house, before the overgrown hedge row, I found Lisa Nanner humming to herself, kneeling over a dirt bed with her back to me. She had on worn, ankle boots with no socks and she wore a sky blue scarf, knotted around her white hair. She wore garden gloves, an old yellow wind-breaker over a dark blue house dress and a tan pair of men's work slacks. I watched her spoon bone meal from a small box into dibbled holes and cover the holes in dirt with her gloved hands.

"Lisa Nanner," I said.

She turned on her knees, a bulb dibble in one gloved hand, a lifted tablespoon dusted with bone meal in the other; her large, black eyes becoming surprised

"Beck," she stared. "Oh...my God."

I tried a smile.

"Oh," she said.

She dropped the bulb dibble and the spoon and I helped her up. She hugged me and began to cry into my jacket.

"Tell me he was a good boy," she said. "Tell me he was a good boy."

"He was," was all I could think to say, trying to think of Foster and the way he was; closing my eyes against the still, bloodied and mutilated image of his bared head in the gray and white snapshot Corporal Pader showed me in Da Nang. I thought of myself with the knife in my sock. I thought of how far I had come to stand here again.

"I-I didn't see you in church," Lisa Nanner said, parting from me with a pained and brave smile. She stepped back, wiped her eyes on her sleeves, her cheeks wet. "I-I was looking for you," she offered. "I was...afraid, too," she admitted with a short laugh and a nod. She hesitated for words. "Everyone at church asked," she rattled on. "Everyone wanted to know where you were...your momma and daddy said you injured yourself?"

I smiled and nodded. "My feet," I said. "Running."

"Your feet?" Lisa Nanner echoed. She looked down at my feet in their dirty chukkas. She shook her head with a puzzled look.

"Where are the dogs?" I asked. "Bosco and Rummy?"

"The dogs?" she said, staring up at me, confused. "Oh, the dogs." She shrugged, sighed. "One died. One ran away. I need to get some more, don't I?" She tried to laugh.

I nodded. "You need dogs in the country," I said.

She smiled and nodded.

"I stayed on another year," I started to tell her, searching her intent and aging face in the knotted scarf, the crinkled corners of her large eyes and the thin teeth of her small smile. I shook my head. "I tried...."

Lisa Nanner nodded and patted my chest with a gloved hand. "I know," she said with a sad and brave smile. "I know. I prayed for you, too, Beck. I did. I prayed for you, too."

I nodded and couldn't think of what else to say.

"Now you come," Lisa Nanner stated, changing the subject, her voice suddenly bright. "You come and see."

"Come and see?"

She smiled and nodded. She took my hand in her gloved one and led me around the house, to the back yard, where I knew there was a line of mulberry trees, the old stone bench, a rusted sundial and a concrete slab hedged in ivory, and the raised and bricked peristyle that held Old Captain Odom's hermetic tomb--a tube capsule, actually--made of white fiberglass, that I recalled came from some company in some place like Snowproof, Florida; and which Foster and I, or my father or Jared Snead, or any of the Fermata Bend veterans, learned to nod to out of respect whenever coming to or going from the Odom's place. Now, Lisa Nanner led me around to the back, to a newer, shiny and parallel capsule beside the Captain's: two, still and white, tube-like shells lying side-by-side on bricked pillars. Engraved into the front, smooth orb of the new one, similar to his father's, was the epithet: *Lance Corporal Arliss Foster Odom, USMC, Born Oct. 12, 1950; Killed In Action in Southeast Asia, August 21, 1970. A Worthy Son. A Worthy Soldier. May He Rest In Peace.*

We stopped before the fiberglass tombs and Lisa Nanner dropped my hand. "Here are my two men," she declared. She paused and smiled up at me beneath her knotted scarf.

"They have left me now," she added, "in some ways...like they always had." She looked to the tombs and sighed. "I come out here in the evenings with a cup of sassafras tea...or sometimes my dinner," her mouth went small, "and I sit here and pray and talk to them...and sometimes I imagine them sailing into eternity," she smiled at me, "contained and whole in these tombs...both of them sailing side-by-side beyond the Flame and the Flood, Beyond the Second Coming and the Big Bang.

"My two men," she said with a soft sigh, "the way I knew them...going into infinity ahead of me, and me always behind them. And that's all right," she said. "I was always brought up to be behind them--a wife and a mother."

Lisa Nanner paused, gave me a quick and chagrined

glance. "Forgive me," she said. "For now, "she added. "For now, what's left of them is here with me."

I nodded and managed a smile for her, trying to imagine what of Foster, from Fermata Bend, Alabama, or the jungles of Vietnam, could be in this fiberglass capsule.

"Where-where's his car?" I asked.

"Car?" Lisa Nanner said.

"You know," I said. "The Mustang."

"Oh," she said, matter-of-fact. She smiled up at me as though it was something silly. "It's in the barn on cinder blocks, Beck. And it'll probably sit there forever," she said.

I nodded.

"Now, you come inside," Lisa Nanner cajoled, changing the subject. She took my arm and peered up at me from under her scarf. "You come inside and I'll fix you something to eat," she declared, "like you and Foster used to do." She tugged at my sleeve. "You come inside, eat and talk to me."

I remembered my manners. I nodded and smiled. "Thank you," I said. "Not today. I-I cant."

"I loved my boy," Lisa Nanner said with a resigned look at me and then to the tombs. She let her hand drop from my arm. "Abbie still comes and visits," she informed me. "She sometimes brings flowers. So did Jane...and Savannah, for a while...and Marica," she looked at me.

"Marica?" I said.

"All the girls," Lisa Nanner smiled. "They loved him, you know? He had so much promise," she paused. "But now, except for Abbie, they don't come anymore," she said. "They've all moved on."

"He'll be in our memories," I said.

"He will always be in mine," Lisa Nanner said.

"Are you okay? You've got help with the place?"

"I'm okay," Lisa Nanner nodded. "My brothers run the fields." She smiled. "I'll get by."

I nodded. I wanted a cigarette bad, but it wasn't the thing to do.

Lisa Nanner smiled and shook her head. "And now I'm to inherit Jared Snead's place, too," she said and sighed. "I'm only kin to dead men." She made a weak laugh.

"What am I going to do with that place?" she said. "Do you want it?"

Back out on the highway, alone with the thrush and pull of the old, hot rod Camaro, I went through the gears and recalled Lisa Nanner's face as she had posed the casual question about Jared Snead's place and how I only smiled and told her no. "Have you been out there?" she had asked. "It's too far gone," she had said with a slow shake of her head. She had looked at me with a sad smile when I told her I had to go. I told her I would come back. "Oh, yes," she had said, nodding, knowing. "Maybe now and then."

Staring at the new blacktop before me and feeling something of what Foster and I were before Vietnam, the old dare came over me. I flicked my cigarette out the window, downshifted into second gear and pushed the accelerator to the floor, through the pain in my foot. The engine screamed. The hood of the car rose. I shifted into third and then fourth and shot down the county highway, roaring toward Fermata Bend, passing two eighteen wheelers and turning back into my lane; speeding under the clear, blue sky; the fall trees of yellow, brown and red leaves; pine thickets and fallow fields choked with sage and golden rods blurring past. I gripped the steering wheel, feeling the power, the freedom and feeling myself grin. I glanced at the rpm gauge and the speedometer, eased off the accelerator at 130 mph, remembering how to coast, slow and downshift into the inertia of the bend in the road before pressing the accelerator again and setting the car into the turn. And I uttered a soft laugh, thinking of Foster as I did that, letting the car slow then to 70 mph. Without a thought and still grinning, I reached for the radio, the automatic motion of an old habit, as if something of me, along with the Byrds or the Monkees, Paul Revere and the Raiders, or maybe Sly and the Family Stone was still alive and on WLS. My revelry and my smile fell while something called "Go Away Little Girl" came on, sung by someone called Donny Osmond. I caught myself, realizing there wasn't any energy for this anymore, the car or the radio, or the road, how everything was strange and indifferent; not special or believable anymore, even if I were to see an old friend or a relative of mine, even if an old song were to come on.

A sudden, flashing, blue bar of light came into my rearview mirror. I stared at a looming, brown sheriff's patrol car in my rearview. I sighed, braked and down-shifted the car, turning the Camaro off onto a grassy shoulder of the road and gradually stopping along a thick line of pine trees. The patrol car pulled behind me, parking on my tail. I cut the engine, closed my eyes and shook my head, remembering how--it seemed long ago--Foster and I used to deliberately do this, only at night and in the next county, with taped license plates--wait until an officer came up to the car and then yell out the window, "Catch me, stupid!" and drive off, laughing and gunning the motor for the back roads, as though the thrill and the challenge of that meant everything.

I opened my eyes. Through the rearview, I watched the

bareheaded, middle-aged officer in the brown patrol car with its flashing top bar light look on me through large, dark and impalpable sunglasses. I watched him write something on a clipboard and call in on his CB radio. I watched him slowly get out of his patrol car and leave the driver's door opened. He set his tan Smokey hat on his head and came up to my side of the car.

I rolled down my window. "Hello, Sheriff Reed," I said.

He stopped and stepped back. He was heavier now, in a brown and tan uniform, still wearing a heavy brown belt with a gun. I noticed the hairs on his sideburns were gray now and his cheeks were fleshier.

"Well, now," Sheriff Reed drawled. "I am a bitches' uncle," he grinned. "If it ain't Beck Senecal, himself. Ha. Son of a--."

He didn't finish, took another step back and took in the car. "Hell, I should have recognized ya," Sheriff Reed declared, laughing with a slow shake of his head. "After all the hell-raising you and ol' Foster used to do. Ha," he said.

He smiled at me. I nodded and smiled, too.

"So, you're back?" he said.

I nodded. The patrol car's top bar light flashed. A pickup truck passed us on the highway.

"Back from Nam," Sheriff Reed whistled. He shook his head slowly. "From the looks of your hair," he said, "I'd say it hasn't been long."

"No sir," I said. "Just back."

"Just back," Sheriff Reed echoed. "Vietnam," he drawled. He looked at me, looked away up the highway, then back at me.

"I'm sorry for that," he said. "I truly am. Sorry about ol' Foster, too. He was a heck of a kid."

"Yes sir," I said, nodding. "He was that."

Sheriff Reed paused. He nodded and sighed. He came slowly forward, rested his arm over the roof of my car, looked away and then down at me.

"It's hard to come back, ain't it?" he said softly. He peeled off his sunglasses and I saw his laughing wrinkles; his calm, dark eyes.

"Yes sir," I admitted. "Truth be told."

He nodded and made a wry smile. "Yeah," he said, "I was that way, too--when I come back from Korea."

He let his hand drop from the hood of my car, holding his sunglasses by the rim in his hand.

"Korea was like..." he said with a frown, "like I had stepped outside myself into hell. And then when I come home," he frowned, "I tried to step back into what I thought I was again."

I nodded. A car passed us and the patrol light flashed.

"Could you?" I said.

Sheriff Reed shook his head and frowned. "I had to bury Korea," he said. "It took a long time. But no," he said. "You'll never quite come back. Close maybe.

"The difference between you and us is," Sheriff Reed went on with a drawl, "is we used to know--or believe--that what we were doing was significant...necessary. It was important. Everyone was in on it," he nodded. "Like gas rationing and war bonds. Rubber and steel drives...everyone paid the price," he paused, "and everyone knew why there was a price to be paid. They'd done it before.

"Now," he muttered, shaking his head, "I don't think anybody knows what we're doing. Men argue about it at the barber shop, watch the war on TV like the weather or the stock market report. It always seems to be somewhere else. We go on with our lives like there's no war and nobody sacrifices...'cept the boys," Sheriff Reed said. He paused and made a wry grin.

"Lord knows," Sheriff Reed said, with a slow and solemn shake of his head, "this county has given more than its share of the boys."

"Yes, sir," I said. "We did what we thought we were supposed to do."

"Every good boy in Escatawpa County doing what is expected of him," Sheriff Reed said. "That's the way of it, ain't it? Like religion," he drawled and paused, "everyone grows up believing what they've been told."

"Yes, sir. That's the way we are," I said. "Like old Jared Snead."

Sheriff Reed laughed. "That old man," he said. "Jared Snead."

Sheriff Reed nodded. "Jared Snead," he echoed. "The Teller of the Tales."

I smiled and nodded. I dug the Zippo lighter out of my jean pocket and lit a cigarette from the pack stuck in my window visor.

"Uh-huh," Sheriff Reed said. "He was our legend all right."

I nodded. Sheriff Reed chuckled. He put on his sunglasses, placed his hands on his hips and sighed.

"All right, now," he drawled, his tone going quiet and serious. "What are we going to do with you?" He paused. "Here I catch you, back in Fermata Bend from Vietnam... your head shaved...I catch you on a casual patrol--in broad daylight and on a Sunday no less," he added, with a shake of his head, "going in reckless excess of speed limit...and with an expired car tag to boot. And...you even *stop*," he added.

Sheriff Reed shook his head in mild exasperation and I had to laugh. When I stopped, I looked at him and took a drag off of my cigarette. I didn't care.

"I've got no excuse, Sheriff," I said. "I got carried away."

Sheriff Reed paused at that. He sighed, shook his head and looked away up the road. When he looked back at me, he let his hands drop from his hips.

"Okay," he drawled. "That's enough. Go on. Get on out of here."

Hey, Becky Boy, Dea's letter read.

Are you surprised I'm writing you? Were you surprised to see me?

It was good to see you, baby, at the train station. That uniform looks good on you. You all grown up, crisp, sharp and cool now. Hey, whatever I said yesterday, don't worry, I'll always remember who you are.

And hey, thanks for that kiss. I'll always remember that. And I think you need to know—pure and simple--that I've always had my eye on you. Always have—ever since I used to watch you and Foster through the screen door where we used to stay down the dirt drive from Jared Snead's place, whenever you brought game to the porch after hunting with Edmond and ya'll would talk and jaw with pappy. Ever since I used to watch you in high school when you weren't looking.

You were my White Dream. And this Is A New Day, Becky. This day you can have and become anything you want to....others may want to go North and go to college and whatever...but all I want to be is somebody in Fermata Bend, Alabama. I want the people I looked up to—to look up at me. Always have. I

*want what Foster was and what you and your kind are—who
know they come from something, have a name and a place and
smile and are kind and know their manners and know they are
a part of something more important than they are. I want to
own that one day, too. I want to buy it all up in my real estate.
I didn't hate you, like some. I wasn't bitter or indifferent, like
some. I want to be like you. You landed families in Fermata
Bend--you old and good ones--got that calm and sure confidence
that don't wash off. You know what you are supposed to be. And
that soldier tradition---It won't shake, neither.*

*Do you remember a story, "Barn Burning," by Faulkner we
read in Mrs. Howard's 11th grade English? Do you remember
it? I read it over and over, and I'm like that boy, Sarty Snopes
who came from nothing, too—only I'm black--but who admired
Major DeSpain's grand old house because, even though it was
built with 'Nigger Sweat,' it stood for people who choose to believe
and practice a peace and a dignity beyond anyone's touch. That's
what I want, too. In my hometown of Fermata Bend. I want to
be the black girl who overcomes and owns it and shows the white
people one better. And be it too. I want all those Fermata Bend
families who I grew up looking up to, who knew who I was, to
know one day I'm one ahead of them. I want to own them. I
want to own it.*

*Call me at Pecan Real Estate. At 288-1103.   Oh, hey,
I know we can't get married or anything. That's too much to ask,
isn't it? But to see you would be nice. Any time.*

Dea

Dea, I scribbled her a quick note before I found a stamp
and an envelope in the kitchen and mailed it from the mailbox on the highway:

Thanks again for bringing me home. You went out of your way.   Dea, whatever it is you think you're talking about— you're crazy. You'd have done better to have read Richard Wright and to have listened to The Supremes or something. Foster and I were blind, Dea. Foster and I, and no telling how may others. We grew up, like children in church, being told and taught and wanting to believe the tales and history, wanting to believe our mothers, our town, our country, and especially the words of our fathers. It's like a spell that's easier to assume than to try and question. You'd best stay away from me. I don't think I know what I am or what I want. I don't think you do, either. Really. If you don't mind, I'm not going to be calling on anyone, okay? I need to be alone. Thanks again and do tell Edmond hello for me. Tell him I'm pulling for him.   Beck

For a moment, then, I thought about writing Marica, too. But when I tried to think of how to say something, or what to say that would be different, I couldn't think of it.

That night, the veterans came while mother cleaned up in the kitchen after dinner and I sat smoking on the sofa of the family room, watching *Love, American Style,* my feet newly bandaged, in clean, thick socks and propped up on the ottoman. I watched as people on the TV smiled or frowned and talked with buoyant, sometimes solemn voices; I noted the timed and enticing glamour of intervening commercials for Wilkerson razor blades, Gillette Foamy, the new American Motors Javelin or Schlitz beer. The doorbell rang three or four separate times. Each time, I heard Dad go to the door from his study and open and close it to the sound of loud, jovial male greeting and talk that quieted and faded as Dad and his friend made their way to his study.

"Where is that boy?" someone declared after a while. I recognized the sound of older male voices, loud and deep, their rising and falling chatter; their voices going muffled with the sound of their footsteps as they came out of the study and into the foyer. I knew from memory how they came to the house, parking their cars and pickup trucks along the chert drive off the highway and walking to our front door in their clean shirts and coats, their weathered faces and their aftershave, with their boasts and their bottles, almost always without their wives: a man thing, a southern man's world, a comradery based on talk, association, the physical and the outdoors; always greeting each other with exclamations and laughs. It was such men who became the childhood stalwarts for Foster and me, and the others. They were the posits, the interpreters of our world. They gave us the impressions and attitudes which we imitated growing up. They instilled what male relationships were, how it was in sports and hunting, and they lent their voices, along with Jared Snead's. We learned of Iwo Jima, the Battle of the Bulge and D-Day. We learned the regional legends of Desoto, Andrew Jackson, Joe Wheeler and Bedford Forrest; we boys memorized their tales, identified them with the mens' faces, with the solemn gravity in the lull of those men's moments at the Co-Op, the drug store, the hardware or the barber shop; around the hunting lodge, Jared Snead's home place and the campfires. The sound of their voices in the house brought back younger memories of Jared Snead, his grinning and his talking, his slow *plinking* of General Beueregard's piano. I remembered the mens' quick winks and grins, the smell of tobacco and whiskey, the smell of wood smoke and damp from hunting coats. The need for loudness and laughter.

The few times the women did come to our house with the men, at Christmas, or even rarer, a dinner party--the men stood off in their suits or sport coats while their wives hugged me at the door in loud, pretty dresses, their hair done, wearing jewelry and makeup. The women exclaimed about other things: my hair, how handsome I was, the time they last saw me. Like instinct, the men, after hellos and nondescript talk, would separate to Dad's study to pour whiskey; the women would wander into the kitchen to chatter and pour sherry. I would be left pretty much to myself then, while the house would fill with talk and tobacco smoke from two ends.

"Where is that boy?"

"In here," I heard Dad answer.

Dad led them into the family room, the men entering behind him, stopping, milling and smiling down at me in the lounge chair. I looked up and saw Mr. Jessups, Mr. Williards, Mr. Little and Mr. Jones.

"Beck!" they grinned and clamored in rough cacophony, motioning to me to stay seated. They stood and looked on, in their clean, casual clothes; the now bare-headed, middle-aged and familiar faces of my childhood. More wrinkles, more glasses, more thinning and graying hair. I nodded and grinned up at them.

"Look who's here! Welcome back!"

Each one stepped forward and gripped my hand, proud and smiling. "A Ranger!" Mr. Jessups declared and slapped my arm, as Mr. Williards did, too. I nodded and grinned and thought I should rise.

"Like your old man!" Mr. Jones said with a nod.

"Like your old man!" someone echoed. "We're proud of you, boy! You fought for us!"

Then came the brief, awkward, smiling silence. They stood and looked on me, while on the TV, a preview of a shooting on a wild west show came on, and then a commercial for Zest soap.

"Say, what happened to your feet?" someone said. The men all held their smiles and looked at dried blood on my socked feet.

"Running," I said.

"He went out and ran his feet raw," Dad told them. He frowned and shook his head.

"Oh?" The other men shook their heads, too, some smiles fading

"Umph," one of them said while a commercial for the new Ford T-bird came on TV.

"Jared Snead would want to see you," Mr. Jones said, nodding with emphasis.

"Yeah, he's the one that would love to see ya," someone said.

I nodded and smiled. They nodded, too. "He would be sorry he missed you," someone said.

Then Mr Williard asked it with a nod: "You glad to be back?" he said. "What was it like?"

I nodded, shrugged. "It was hell," I said, smiling, unable to think of any other way to say it to the confident men of my childhood, unable to say what the war in Vietnam was truly for or if that it was being won.

The men all looked on me and nodded, respectful, middle-aged, quiet; removed and somehow helpless. What was happening in Vietnam was beyond them.

"We'll win it," one of them said.

They nodded in that old confidence of theirs, standing there with Dad and looking at me.

"It's a hard war," someone commented. "But we'll win." A nod. "Americans always win."

I looked at them. No one mentioned Foster, Curtis, Johnny or Bubba. I managed to nod, give some simple answers and smile. They nodded, then grinned and waved as they followed Dad out of the family room, leaving me alone with a commercial for Lavoris mouthwash on the TV and a brief network announcement that the latest on the war in Southeast Asia would be aired tonight.

Later, I limped into the kitchen and startled my mother at the counter.

"Mom," I smiled.

"Oh," Mom stepped back. She forced a smile.

She had cleaned up the kitchen and the day's dishes and was arranging cheese, Nabisco crackers and ham bits on a large platter. The muffled banter and laughter of the men drifted in now and then from the Dad's study, along with the smell of cigarette smoke.

"Mom," I took a breath. "Listen, yesterday…"

"No, no, no," she shook her head, forcing a quick smile. "I don't want to know." She turned back to the platter. "I don't want to know," she trilled. A distance came into her face, her smile. She kept busy.

"I didn't mean to," I said. "It just happened."

She gave me a quick look. Tears brimmed in her eyes. "I know, I know," she said. "You're my boy." She nodded too fast, trying not to be scared, smiling. "You're my boy," she said.

"Yeah. I'm your boy," I said. I watched her, not knowing what else to say, forgetting exactly what I meant to do by coming into the kitchen and remembering how my parents came home that evening after I had parked the Camaro in the shed and returned the battery to Dad's International pickup, how they found me alone in the dark house in my hunting jacket and socked feet, smoking and seated in the lounge chair of the family room before the eery and shifting glow of Harry Reasoner in black and white, who was talking on *Sixty Minutes* on TV. Mom and Dad turned on the lights in the house and they stood smiling in the doorway with their coats on, both talking at once and telling me how everyone they had seen that day wanted to see me, missed me, and wanted to know how I was. I looked up, nodded and smiled, told them I was sorry and that I would go later sometime.

"And when will that be?" Mom said.

I shrugged.

They went quiet at that. Dad took their coats to the closet and Mom stayed, looking on in the doorway, holding her smile. She finally asked if I wanted something to eat, averting her gaze from me as she waited on my answer. I realized then how they had hurried into the house.

"Sure," I said to her, remembering to smile. "Sure. I'll eat something."

Dad came back to the doorway, winking and grinning at me. I smiled and nodded to try and be one of them. On TV, we watched Harry Reasoner, his nonplused face and a level stare, give a solemn spiel of facts on the cost of living, population growth and air pollution, then came clips of Golda Meir, Nixon and Kissinger, clips of anti-war protests in Boston, Cleveland and San Diego. Mother left for the kitchen and Dad lingered in the doorway.

"How was your day?" he said.

I started to say something, but a clip of recent war action showed and we both watched. A large scale map of Vietnam came on with graphic fire flashes of where action had been. Harry Reasoner stated the week's American death count at twenty-nine; the enemy body count at a hundred or more, his words as flat, matter-of-fact and as intangible as the statistics of car wrecks, the weather or the price of bacon.

"Um-mph," Dad said. He shrugged and shook his head.

I nodded and looked back to the TV. When I looked to him again, he was not in the doorway.

Now, standing in the kitchen in an awkward silence, my mom suddenly turned and handed me the platter.

"Here," she said, insisting with a knowing and quiet finality. "You should be with the men."

The men all turned as I limped into the study with the platter. "C'mon in!" they declared in disjointed and loud voices. I entered their banter, their tobacco smoke, their wrinkles and smiling demeanors, their drinks in their hands. They slapped me on the back. Someone took the platter from me and put it on Dad's desk. Someone else put a glass of sour mash and ice into my hand. "How are ya, boy?" they chorused. "Ready to do some deer hunting?" "You ready to run some foxes?"

I nodded, smiled, watched their aged faces, waited until they resumed talking among themselves about Governor Brewer, the price of soybeans and hay, how the first freeze had come early. In football, 'Bama was running the Wishbone, Pat Sullivan at Auburn was throwing The Bomb. I listened, standing, back among their voices again, the hometown veterans, my mentors who had been mentored, in turn, by the likes of my grandfather and Jared Snead.

I nodded and smiled out of respect to their faces and voices, sipped sour mash, lit my cigarettes and theirs on my Zippo. Now and then, one of the men would give me a slap on the shoulder, then a look with a pause. "All right! Atta boy!" No one said, "Foster" or "Vietnam". It was too alien. It was not clear. It was strange and taboo. Instead of saying the strange and taboo, they repeated themselves, each one saying something else, each one telling me how proud of me he was. Because we were American. Because America was Right. Each reminded me in a whisper how he had served in either Europe, the South Pacific or Korea. I nodded, making my smiles brief, remembering their voices again, their sanguine, younger faces in my childhood, remembering Foster, too, and how many times we had both heard their stories before.

"Jared Snead," Mr. Jones hugged my neck, his words slurred with sour mash. "He would love to see ya," he cried. His reddened face went sad. "He'd be so proud," Mr. Jones said. "He would say so."

I nodded. "We miss him," I said.

I looked at them, aging men with reddening faces and loose tongues in a haze of tobacco smoke, feeling a slow and creeping Disconnect from them. The essence of whatever I was, whatever I had done, had nothing to do with them.

At some point The Disconnect overcame me. "I miss Foster," I blurted into the hum of their voices. They hushed. They turned to me. Some looked away.

"He was a good boy," my dad said, from across the room. The men nodded.

I raised my glass. The men slowly raised theirs.

"Why doesn't anyone want to say his name?" I said. "To Foster Odom," I declared. "One of us, the best of us." I thought of Marica, too, and I felt my throat go tight.

"To Foster Odom," the men of my childhood repeated to me. "The best of us." They nodded. They drank after I did.

I became lost in the steady drone of the men's voices after that, their words, their ever proud smiles and winks, my father's ever proud smile and wink. I thought of Bubba Smith, Johnny Newsome and Curtis Johnson, too, and I went limping out of the study, into the frost green family and living rooms, turning off the TV and the lights because the rooms seemed vacant and too bright; and feeling strangely taut in the face, tired and numb, and feeling as though I was in something like a slow vertigo, the hum of the older mens' voices carrying in my ears, something about a march for Jared Snead--while recalling the warm, inclusive and familiar presence of them in my childhood; their security, the way they slapped my shoulder and gripped my hand tonight, as though I now had earned the right to be one of them. *All right! Atta boy!* I saw Jared Snead grinning at me with his unkempt beard and tobacco-stained teeth, in his battered fedora. I remembered how he shook my hand outside the post office before I left for Vietnam. I heard the mens' praises and shouts in the woods when I killed my first buck. I heard their cheers from the bleachers as I played in baseball games.

I stopped and stood in the dark of the living room and stared out the front window to the night and the highway, feeling the slow, dull throbbing in my feet, recalling the ever-constant rhythm of the train from California and see-ing my platoon buddies spread out in the field, their helmets and strained faces; feeling now that I was deserting them and recalling that desperate fear of deserting Foster's memory; and whether right or wrong, being able to live with myself and my memory in Fermata Bend, too.

Something of Marica came to me: her long, red hair; the steady, calm stare of her grey eyes. I suddenly wanted to hobble out to my Camaro, drive up to her house and pound on the front door under that old yellow stoop light until she would come out in something like a bathrobe, blinking and surprised. *I'm sorry. I'm sorry. I love you,* I'd shout. *You love me?* I would hear her echo, would see her in a staring, ponder of doubt. And there I would be: Too Late and an outsider now, reduced to shame because I had given myself up to be worthy of one thing, while not being worthy of the other. Then I imagined if her fiancé, Roddy Sexton, or her parents were there, I would only be reduced to awkward manners, could only stare, nod; but worse, I feared seeing nothing left of us in her eyes, nothing left of the look I knew before Foster died, before her last letter, before I slit VC guards' throats in the nights of my anger, before the death of Jared Snead, "The Teller of The Tales" in Fermata Bend, Alabama.

"Beck, my boy," Dad said. "Are you there?"

I turned and saw my father, out of the study and the soft, humming talk of Fermata Bend men, standing under the small ceiling light of the foyer, the collar of his shirt unbuttoned, a glass in his hand. He was trying to see me, peering into the dark of the living room; a tentative, wry smile.

"Yeah, Dad," I answered after a pause. "Yeah, I'm here."

After Mom's dinner, Walter Cronkite on CBS and more news of the dead in Vietnam, I watched *Bewitched* with my parents in the family room. We sat together on the sofa, seeing the same commercials I had been seeing for days, except for one with a road construction crew in the heat imagining an ice cold Coca Cola in the refrigerator, "back behind the mayonnaise". The sweaty, dirty men on the crew made dry swallows and then ran for their trucks. Like all of the commercials, it had bold letters, people and song. My feet were better. That afternoon, I had put on socks and boots and helped Dad cut up logs and haul debris wood to fill-in a gully in the pasture. We said little. Dad eyed me and smiled now and then.

Ever since my run up the road, my parents and I hadn't talked much. Mom kept up a bright, quick, talkative front, but without questions, usually in the kitchen after I slept late in the mornings, ate and then left for the family room to watch cooking shows and soaps on TV. When Dad came home, he smiled and winked and said too much about nothing, too. The moments I was alone with my mother or my father, I felt their pauses and felt like neither one of us knew how to begin.

In the middle of a Crystal Oil commercial with a smiling, brunette women holding a can of the product in a kitchen while a male background voice talked about cooking, the phone rang. Mom rose from the sofa and went out into the hallway to answer it while Dad and I remained seated, waiting for Elizabeth Montgomery to come back on with her shoulder-length, curled, blonde hair and dark eyebrows, waiting for her to wiggle her petite nose to freeze Darren, so he couldn't say rude things.

Mom came back and stood in the doorway. "It's for you, Beck."

"Me?"

"Yes, you," she said, nodding at me with a puzzled look. "I couldn't understand him though."

I rose from the sofa, went past her, into the hallway and to the phone nook. I picked up the receiver. "Hello?" I said. I couldn't make out who it was until the person told me again.

"Beck, it's me, man," he exclaimed. "Joe...er, Joey McDowell." His old accent was gone. His voice came eager and flat over the phone. His words were evenly paced.

"Is this Beck Senecal?" Joey repeated.

"Yes. Joey," I laughed. "What the hell are you doing back in Fermata Bend?"

"Beck," he exclaimed. "Long time, man." He paused, laughed, and even his laughter sounded flat. "Sorry to call you like this," he said. "But my old lady said you were back."

"Yeah," I said. "Yeah."

"Me and my new girl just dropped in from Atlanta, man," Joey said. "That's when my old lady told me you were back from Nam." He whistled. "Jeez, man. Foster and Curtis dead, Bubba MIA. I can't believe it. How are *you,* man?"

I told him I was okay. I didn't want to talk about that.

Instead, we talked about other things. He told me about his job as a DJ in Atlanta. We reminisced on high school days, light and trivial things, where other people had gone. How long had I been back? Was I glad to be home?

Joey's voice didn't change. He had been in the same year with Foster and me in high school, had played summer league baseball with us, baled hay and hunted with us some. Joey had tried to enlist Deferred Entry his senior year, too, in typical, old Fermata Bend family fashion, just like the rest of us. But he had failed his physical with an irregular heart beat. He had gone straight to broadcasting school in Birmingham after that and found work fast.

"Hey, man," Joey said. "That's still a bummer on Foster and Curtis and Bubba. I get sad when I think about it, man. Y'all--er, *you* were all my heroes, man."

He paused and I felt myself nod.

"Hey, man, I want to see you, okay?" Joey said, his eager and flat voice back. "I've got a surprise for you, too. Can you come out?"

I thought about it for a moment. Joey was from the old days. "Yeah, okay," I said. "I can come out there."

"Far out, man!"

I hung up and went back into the family room where Mom and Dad sat on the sofa before the TV watching a Chevy commercial of a new Corvette winding down a curving road above the ocean.

"Who was that?" Mom looked up.

"Joey McDowell," I told her.

"*That* was Joey McDowell?" Mom shook her head at me with an incredulous look. "I didn't recognize him," she said.

"Neither did I," I admitted. "But it would be good to see him. Could I borrow the car?"

"Oh," Dad shrugged with a slow smile. "Sure," he said. He rose from the sofa and fished into his pants pockets. "Joey McDowell, you say?"

I nodded.

"Well, have fun," Dad said. He found and handed me the keys. He looked at the TV. "When you see Joey," he added, "tell him about that march we've got planned for Jared Snead."

"That march?"

"Yeah, the march," Dad said. "You remember," he turned his eyes from the TV to me. "Me and the boys were talking about it with you the other night," he smiled. "We're going to march on Veterans' Day, then stand guard at Jared Snead's grave." Dad nodded. "Remember?"

"Oh, yeah," I said. "Oh, yeah?"

"And you're going, right?" Dad smiled at me, his look expectant. "Wear your uniform? Make us all proud?"

"Oh, yes," Mom pitched in. "People will see you for a change. You need to get out," she said.

"Oh," I said. I held the keys and looked from Dad to Mom, then back to Dad. They looked at me and not the TV.

"I don't think so," I said. "I don't think I will."

My parents held their looks on me. Dad's mouth closed into a thin line.

"What? How can you not?" he said, staring at me in disbelief. A chipper voice came from the TV talking about Reynolds Aluminum.

"I'm sorry. I can't." I looked at him. I didn't feel proud. I didn't want to talk to anyone who was proud.

My parents stared and said nothing. The TV began a show.

"Thanks for the keys," I said to their silent faces. I nodded and out of old habit, I went and kissed Mom on the cheek before I left, remembering how kissing her was once a familiar thing to do, what I used to do when I was in high school, and right before she would tell me not to stay out too late.

I thought of Joey as I drove my parents' Oldsmobile 88 in a light drizzle to the McDowells' house, wearing an old windbreaker of mine I found in the foyer closet. Even in high school, Joey was more into music and disc jockeying than Foster and I were, listening to the radio all the time and imitating the DJs. "It's the real, man," he used to say. "It's where it's at--*out* of here," he would laugh. The last time I saw him was during my leave before Nam, at his sister, Kathy's wedding in church. Joey came with his parents and wore a suit. He smiled and hugged me like everyone else. Everyone smiled. Marica was in the wedding and so was Abbie. Foster and Bubba were there, too, but Curtis Johnson was overseas.

In high school, Joey, like me and the others, wore longer hair, bell bottoms, Dino boots, wide belts; loud shirts with big collars and cuffs. We played high school baseball and some-times fished and hunted together. We mended fences and baled hay for spending money. We boys hung out together on weekend nights and after dates around the town square or on the back roads where we raced our cars and drank bootleg beer. Unlike our fathers and mothers, who grew up listening

to country or Big Band music, and maybe Elvis--we Fermata
Bend boys learned to listen to rock. It was new, it was happening. I could remember singing to songs on Joey's custom
radio and eight-track sound system in his Malibu while we all
parked along the river. Joey mimicked the DJs. He would
even time their intros and commercials with a stopwatch. He
would grin at us and name each song.

I turned into the chert drive that ran through pasture to
the McDowells' bricked house, the house lights on through
the pecan trees. I parked the car in the drive, went up the
steps in the rain to the front door and rang the doorbell, waiting with a grin, anticipating Joey; but it was Mr. McDowell
who answered, in worn overalls and a work shirt, balding
now, smaller than I remembered him.

"How you doing, boy?" He grinned and shook my hand.
"Glad you're back, son! Glad you're back!"

"Fine, Mr. McDowell," I smiled. "Thank you."

Mr. Dowell looked at my head, took my windbreaker and
asked about my mom and dad. He said he and his wife had
missed me at church, that they had met my parents a few days
before at the post office.

"Your mother's a lady, now," Mr. McDowell stated with a
smile.

"Yes sir. Thank you."

Mr. McDowell slapped me on the back and led the way
into the dining room. Everyone looked up from the large
oak table. Joey was seated on the other side with a small,
bright blonde girl who met me with steady black eyes. Mrs.
McDowell was seated at the far end. Joey and Mrs. McDowell both smiled at me. Mrs. McDowell was in a simple blue
house dress. She had gained weight since I had left for Nam
and her hair looked too black. Joey and his girlfriend were

drinking from liqueur glasses. On the table before them was an ashtray, a wadded ball of gift wrapping paper and a bottle of Brandy and Benedictine with a bright red ribbon around the neck. Joey was smoking. His brown hair was long now, to his waist, and held out of his face in a leather headband. There was loud rouge on his cheeks and he wore a dark brown sport coat over a yellow sweat shirt with a colored screen print of an opened mouth.

I remembered my manners and went to Mrs. McDowell first. I took her hand when she offered it. She smiled at me and even seemed relieved. She pulled me down to her, hugged me and kissed me on the cheek.

"Oh, good to see you, Hon," she said. "Good to have you back."

"You, too," I smiled.

Joey rose and gave me a firm handshake across the table, his smile all teeth. I saw he had on wide-legged, yellow slacks, too. We grinned at one another.

"How are you?" I said.

"All right, man. *Man*," he said. "You look, well, crisp... fit," he laughed. "I hardly recognized you on the phone."

"Same here."

The girl rose from the table and offered her hand. Mrs. McDowell blinked at her in surprise.

"I'm Caren," she said.

I nodded, took her hand. "Beck."

She made a face. "Joey tells me you're just back from that ...that *carnage* we hear on the news," she said. She eyed me with a frown, stared at my hair.

"Yes," I said. I tried a grin. "I'm back."

"Oh," she said, her tone morose. Her face was as smooth and shiny as plastic. She had large black eyes; long hair;

mauve, wet-look lipstick, matching mascara and nails. She was wearing a white oxford blouse, first three buttons open, revealing three or four gold necklaces dangling various sized gold unicorns, and red, plastic hot pants with white panty hose.

"Have a drink," Joey said, holding his smile.

Mr. McDowell waved to the chair in front of me and he got me a glass from the cupboard. He placed it on the table before me, took the end chair opposite Mrs. McDowell and we all sat down. Joey pushed the bottle toward me.

"We brought this with us from Atlanta to keep us warm, man." He winked. "But Mom and Dad don't want any."

"Are you hungry, Hon?" Mrs. McDowell asked. "You want something to eat?"

I poured myself a drink. "Thank you," I gave her a smile. "But I've eaten."

"I fixed his favorite supper," Mrs. McDowell told me, nodding toward Joey, her tone playful but miffed. "And he didn't want it."

"We ate fast food along the way," Joey commented.

"These are my boys, Hon," Mrs. McDowell continued, finding Caren with a slow smile. "I raised them with the cows and the corn." She reached out and squeezed my arm. "They're *mine*, honey." She tried a laugh. I smiled back. Caren tried Mrs. McDowell's smile and looked everyone over.

"Joey, Beck and Fost—" Mr. McDowell caught himself, paused. "Joey and Beck," he tried again to Caren with a smile, "they were among the best outfielders Fermata Bend ever had."

I looked at Mr. McDowell, suddenly overcome with sadness, and I couldn't say anything.

Caren stared at me, then Mr. McDowell. "Wow," she said. "Strange."

"Foster," Joey insisted with a solemn nod. "Foster, Beck and me--we were hell now." He made a thin smile and a shake of his head. "I would have been one of you, too, man, if I'd passed that physical," he said. "I would have gone with you, too."

"Can you believe it?" Caren whispered, becoming wide-eyed. "*You all,*" she looked everyone over and paused. "*You all* have grown up together, touched each other's lives, in that--like, you know--that kindred spirit," she found the words, sighed. "*You all* have grown up in this small place."

Mr. and Mrs. McDowell stared at her. Joey looked away with a smirk. I took a quick sip of my drink.

"That's it, baby," Joey said. He nodded, grinned and rubbed his cigarette out in the ashtray.

"Amen," Mr. McDowell offered with a soft laugh.

"Amen," Caren echoed, as if learning how to say it.

I lit a cigarette on my Zippo. Joey pushed the ashtray toward me, slid his arm around Caren and shot her a smile.

"Caren's a model," Joey informed me. "From New York, man. She's doing a three week stint in 'Lanta for I'll Be Truckin' clothes that we are supposed to be wearing down here." He grinned at me. "I brought her home so she could see what Small Town South looks like."

Caren clasped her hands. "My first time every," she said to me. "*You all* have so much land down here."

Joey grinned at her. Mr. and Mrs. McDowell smiled after he did.

"You're right, Hon," Mrs. McDowell said, "there's plenty of that."

"Fresh air," Mr. McDowell offered.

"How do you do it?" Caren stared at Mr. McDowell. "How can you stand it?"

Mr. McDowell blinked, shrugged. He kept smiling. "This is it," he said. "We have our ways."

"Amen," Caren said with a laugh. "*You all* know each other, have common values and go to church all the time."

"We look out for each other," Mr. McDowell said.

Caren covered her ears. "I don't believe what I'm hearing!" Her voice was shrill. "An old, decadent culture!" She turned her eyes on me. I looked at her face and took a drag off my cigarette. I leaned back in my chair, toyed with my glass and turned toward Mr. McDowell to give her my best side, and I smiled in what I thought was my calm, confident way.

"Were you a Crimean soldier?" she said.

"A what?" I looked at her. Her gaze was steady. Joey grinned.

"Er, no. I was in Vietnam."

"No, no, silly," she scolded. "Before that. In the other life."

No one laughed. Mrs. McDowell studied her hands as she folded them on the table. Joey caught Caren's eye and gave her a wink. Still grinning, he took a platinum case from inside his coat. I watched him remove a long, filtered cigarette and light it with a platinum lighter. He waved the cigarette in his hand.

"Caren's got ESP," he informed me. "She's a medium, man."

I looked from him to her. She was staring me in. I looked back at Joey.

"It's not in right now," Joey continued, "but it's true. Last week we were shopping along Peachtree, for example," he took a drag off his cigarette, "and right in the middle of the sidewalk, man, she drops her bags, her eyes roll back into her head and she starts shaking and freaking out. She saw the street as dirt and mud, became a little girl screaming for her mother in a burning wood building. Her name was Sarah," Joey said. "She said, 'Momma'. Stuff like that." Joey looked at her and took a calm drag on his cigarette. Caren kept her eyes on me. Mr. and Mrs. McDowell held small smiles.

"That so?" I said. I took a sip of my drink and took a drag on my cigarette.

"Our trip down," Joey continued, "she gaped out the car window at the woods and countryside, became a Confederate soldier bleeding to death, begging for water as we went by a battlefield that's now nothing but asphalt, she reiterated the conversations and cries of people before two car wrecks--just as I was getting into Emerson, Lake and Palmer's "Lucky Man" on the radio, man--and a couple screwing in a sleeping bag out in a field under the moon."

Mrs. McDowell squirmed in her seat and looked away. Caren made a slow grin.

"Then a hitchiker playing "Orange Blossom Special" on a harmonica," Joey went on, "while walking down the interstate in a thunderstorm. Real psycho," he said, taking a calm drag off his cigarette. I pushed the ashtray toward Joey so we could share it.

Caren's eyes had not left me.

"Do you sometimes feel a twitch, a pulsating feeling on your left side?" she said.

I glanced to Mr. and Mrs. McDowell, looked at her. "Well, yes," I said. "Sometimes."

"In your past life," she said, "you were a Crimean soldier," her eyes didn't move, "French, I think. You were killed at the Battle of Balaklava with a bayonet in your left side."

"Did it hurt?" I said.

Joey laughed. Mr. and Mrs. McDowell made the same smiles. Caren ignored them and watched me. I avoided her look, sipped my drink and smoked my cigarette, seeing then the scarlet mush of Private Dupre's face as he did die, in the red-tinged dirt of Vietnam, staring at me with one still, blue eye. *Take me home,* he had sighed on his last breath.

"Well, say," I asked Joey to change the subject, dispel the thought, "how is the mike-mouthing?"

Joey squashed his cigarette out in the ashtray. He nodded. "Great man," he said. "Rod Stewart, Jackson Five, Three Dog Night fighting for the top, then The Temptations," his voice quavered with eagerness, "Cat Stevens, and Edgar Winter, chased by Santana and Hot Tuna. McDonald's has a good hitting ad, man, and Coke's done a catching new commercial."

"I've heard that one," Mrs. McDowell said. She hesitated. "'It's the real thing?'"

"No, Mom," Joey frowned, "that one's old. The new one for Christmas is 'I'd Like to Buy the World a Coke.'" Joey looked at us, grinned. He sang the first bar.

"Oh," Mrs. McDowell said.

"It changes," Mr. McDowell laughed.

"Two weeks ago, we had a promotion gimmick," Joey told me, his voice continuing excited. "The teenies loved it, man. Get this," he said, "we had a 'Are you Kink or Funk?' contest." He grinned at everyone. "We kept score. The kids called in, gave their votes, names and addresses, and we checked them off the phone book. *Two thousand calls* in five days, man. Two thousand calls. We kept posting the returns on the air. We put every one hundredth caller on the air, too, talked to him or her a bit. If he was for Kink, he got a free ticket to see The Kinks; if he was for Funk, he got a free ticket to see Sly and the Family Stone. We announced the winner the following Saturday. Funks won it, 1253 to 759."

Joey shook his head, laughed. "A riot, man. The kids eat that stuff up."

Caren giggled. Mr. and Mrs. McDowell smiled. I saw Mrs. McDowell catch Mr. McDowell's eye and nod. They slowly rose from the table. I squashed my cigarette in the ashtray and started to rise, too. Mrs. McDowell smiled and waved me back down.

"No, no," she said with a nod. "It's all right."

"We're going to let y'all talk," Mr. McDowell said.

"*Ya-all?*" Caren echoed.

Mr. and Mrs. McDowell kept smiling. "Help yourselves to anything," Mrs. McDowell said and looked at Caren. "Your room is ready," she smiled. They slowly pushed their chairs under the table. Caren waved as Mr. McDowell waited on Mrs. McDowell. They left the kitchen together toward the family room.

"Bet you're going to watch *Lawrence Welk*," Joey said after them. The corners of his mouth turned down in mock scorn.

Caren giggled. I smiled. We poured new drinks.

"How are things your way?" Joey asked. He paused. "How are you, man?"

I shrugged, didn't answer.

"You look hard," Caren shuddered. "Like a robot."

I tried a smile. I shook my head and sipped my drink.

"Bad, huh?" Joey said. "Man," he shook his head, "who would have believed what a bad rap it's become? The Tet Offensive," he said, shaking his head. "Mai Lai. It's a bum deal, man. And we were all gung ho."

"We won Tet," I said.

Joey shook his head at me. "You wouldn't know it...to

hear the media...the people up North and in California. It all just seems...irrelevant." He made a sad laugh. "And down here, we pretty much keep doing what we've always done."

"I guess so," I said.

"You know so. You and Foster, man," Joey said with a sad grin, "Curtis and Bubba. I loved y'all, man. And I would have been one of you, too, man." He shook his head.

"*Ya-all?*" Caren tried.

"Y'all...*you*..." Joey said to me, "are trying to hold up that old guard, man. God, and country," he sighed. "Duty, man. Manhood. Christ," Joey shook his head. "We are fools. We Southerners are great fools."

"I don't know that," I said.

"Oooh," Caren singsonged, staring at both of us. "Are you and Beck like, you know, *fools?*"

"Definitely," Joey said. He raised his glass. I didn't comment or raise my glass.

"But to you," Joey said, "and the others."

"The others," I said and raised my glass.

Caren smiled and raised her glass. We drank. Joey gulped his drink down, nodding to me. Caren imitated Joey's nod to me and giggled. Joey gave Caren a wink.

In silence, Joey poured us new drinks. Joey and I lit new cigarettes and Caren smiled and hummed to herself. Joey brought up favorite movies. "The best were *Shaft* and *Play Misty for Me,*" he said with a nod and a grin. Caren voiced for *Honky* and *The Seven Minutes.*

"Honky?" Joey and I said and stared at her. Caren squealed.

Both Caren and Joey liked *The Omega Man* and *The Summer of '42.* I smiled. I hadn't seen those films, hadn't been in their world. I drank and listened to them talk, beginning to feel the liqueur. In Nam, during R&R there were USO shows, but old films and cheap girlie flicks. Nothing memorable.

Watching Joey and Carens' faces, I recalled how, before Nam, Foster and I double-dated in one of our hot rods to movies at the Cherokee Drive-In on the road to Citronelle. We would race other cars along the way. Marica and Abbie. Popcorn, cokes and laughter. Box speakers in the car windows. And if the girls were not there, bragging and bootleg beer. I remembered myself making out with Marica in the dark back seat of Foster's Shelby Cobra Mustang before Natalie Wood's wide brown eyes on the larger than life, cimascoped screen, and to piped sounds from the window speakers. I saw Abbie with her longer hair, making out with Foster in the front seats under John Wayne's grin.

"Hey."

Joey and Caren were staring at me. "What's happening, man?" Joey said.

I shrugged and smiled. "Sorry."

Joey shook his head. "We're on favorite TV shows, man," he grinned. "What's yours?"

I shrugged. I listened while Joey liked *Columbo* and *All in The Family*. Caren liked *Night Gallerie*. Joey nodded. "Yeah, that was good. Far out," he said. I hadn't seen either of them. Best TV Shows of all time. I opted for the *Andy Griffith Show*. Joey and Caren nodded. Joey liked *I Love Lucy*. Caren vouched for *Long Hot Summer*.

"What?" Joey and I made faces. We booed her.

"That's the way I wanted to picture the South," she giggled.

"*The Gray Ghost*," Joey and I both remembered in unison, laughing.

"Gray who?" Caren frowned.

It was a boyhood favorite, we explained to her, like *Combat!* And *Twelve Oclock High.*

"Only it didn't play anywhere but in the South," Joey told her.

"Oh," she said. "Why not?"

"Because only Southerners want to watch themselves fight in the Civil War," Joey laughed.

"Oh, wow," Caren said. "You mean, the significance of your history?"

Joey and I laughed.

"I'm afraid we know about that better than you do," I said.

We laughed and we kept going. We all liked *Man From UNCLE* and *Batman.* Favorite TV commercials. I didn't know the latest ones. Joey liked Schick commercials. Caren liked Dial.

Best TV commercials of all time. Joey sang and imitated Edie Adams for Muriel cigars: "Why don't you pick one up and smoke it, some time?" Caren liked the Starkist Charlie Tuna commercials. "Tell 'em Charlie sent ya," her voice broke into a squeal. Joey and I shook our heads. She also liked the "Daisy" spot campaign ad LBJ used to beat Goldwater in the '64 election. Joey and I stared at her while she pretended to pluck petals, sounding out a count-down and then a big explosion, puffing her cheeks out and letting her hands rise and fall for the nuclear cloud on the TV screen.

She paused. "Didn't...didn't *ya-all* get that down here?" She stared at us.

Joey and I laughed. We poured new drinks. We were getting drunk. I lit everyone's cigarette on my Zippo. Caren held her eyes on me as I lit hers. I kept finding the point of

the "V" on her unbuttoned blouse while Joey brought up
more old commercials. Joey imitated the one by Volkswagon
in the sixties with the long funeral procession of weeping
people in large, expensive cars to the solemn sound of a voice
reading a Last Will and Testament, then last in the procession
was the thrifty nephew in a VW bug who inherited the entire
estate. Joey imitated the nephew who dabs his eyes, but then
smiles. We laughed. Caren asked if we knew a Mr. Clean
commercial. Joey and I couldn't remember. I reiterated
"Can't Believe I Ate the Whole Thing," and then the commercial with prisoners chanting for Alka Seltzer. Caren asked if
we could remember the Brylcreem commercials, but Joey and
I couldn't remember. We poured new drinks, I lit everyone's
cigarette on my Zippo. Caren kept her eyes on me.

In the middle of my rendition of a Benson and Hedges
commercial--the one with the explorers trapped in the Egyp-
tian tomb and only one last cigarette, "Benson and Hedges
lasts a long, long time," Caren nudged Joey, gave him a look.
Joey put his arm around her and kissed her hair.

"What time is it?" he asked me.

I stopped, looked at my watch. "Jesus," I said. "It's
twenty-three thirty-two...er, eleven thirty-two," I said.

"I promised Caren I'd show her some sights," Joey said.

"What? Sights?" I looked at him. I stifled a laugh.

"Yeah," Joey grinned, "thought I'd show her Jared Snead's
place. You know. He's dead now and everything...and it's
vacant."

"Jared Snead's place? Now?" I echoed, seeing his old,
rough beard; his grin and his battered fedora. "Why?"

Joey grinned, shrugged. "Caren wants to see some South,
man," he said. "Hey, we won't hurt anything."

"Oh, please?" Caren cried. "Won't you?" She clasped her

hands together and gave Joey and me a long, imploring look. "Please? I want to know it," she said. "I want to know."

I thought then to tell Joey about the Veterans' Day march, but I thought better of it.

"It's just an old house," Joey stated. "C'mon," he said to me. "We won't do anything. It's going to Probate, anyway."

"I've got to go to the bathroom," Caren said.

Joey and Caren got up from the table. I slowly rose with them. We downed our drinks. Joey took the bottle. The rest of the house was quiet and dark.

"You sure about this?" I said.

"Yeah, we're sure," Joey said. "Folks must have gone to bed," he observed. He cautiously led us into the dark hallway and to the bathroom, found the bathroom light switch and flipped it on.

"No peeking through the key hole," Caren whispered to us with a giggle. She went in and shut the door. Joey and I waited and took nips from the bottle.

"Good to see you, man." Joey grinned. "Been a long time."

I smiled. "She's good looking," I told him.

"She's good, too," Joey winked. "She takes me high, you know? She's fast. She's easy. No commitment shit."

I nodded and I remembered Vin Trough.

When Joey took his turn, Caren leaned against the door frame and stared me in with a silly smile. "*You-all* are *sooo* sweet," she said, almost in a singsong. "Soft and sweet." She laughed. "I can't get over *you-all*. I can't wait to see what *you-all* grew up in."

We shared the bottle. "The word's *y'all*," I said.

"Oh," Caren said. She stifled a giggle with her hand.

After I went to the bathroom, Joey led us down the hallway to the closet across from Mr. and Mrs. McDowell's bedroom door. He put a finger to his lips for silence and Caren stifled a giggle. We got our coats out of the closet, my windbreaker, Joey's trench coat, Caren's red, ankle-length cashmere. Joey found a flashlight. Caren giggled.

"Ssssh," Joey and I said together. She giggled louder. Joey clamped his hand over her mouth, led the way through the living room and out the front door. Outside was dark and wet, but the stars were out. I shut the door softly behind us. Joey let go of Caren's mouth and they French kissed before me on the front steps, their breaths steaming. Then Joey led the way down the steps to a small, dark car and unlocked both doors.

"What is this?" I said. "I've never seen it."

"It's a Datsun Z," Joey laughed. "It's Japanese."

"Japanese?" I said. I shook my head at the car in disbelief. "Japanese?"

I crawled into the tight backseat of the car with the bottle. Joey got in behind the wheel and Caren took the front passenger's side.

"Hey, Joey," Caren whispered, after we shut the doors, "before we see that South of yours, you...you got any stuff?"

Joey laughed. "No, sugar," he said. "And I could use a toke, myself. Beck?" Joey grinned at me in the rearview. "You got, man?"

"Don't look at me," I shook my head.

Caren sighed. "Well then, I want a cigarette," she said.

Joey flipped the platinum case to her. She fished out a cigarette, looked at him. "I don't have a light," she said.

"On the dash," Joey reported as he started the car.

Caren gave him a long look. "That wasn't the way you treated me on the way down here," she said. "You were a ...*gentleman,*" she stressed with a silly grin.

I reached over from the back seat and flicked her a light on my Zippo.

"Thank *you*," Caren said. She lit her cigarette and giggled.

Joey turned on the headlights, drove away from the house, down the drive and onto the silent, wet county highway with the heater on, the wipers going slow speed; the headlights of the car seeming like small, dual prods against the night. Caren cracked open her window and smoked, smiling to herself, hugging her coat and looking out the window. We passed the bottle around. Joey kept his hand on Caren's knee when he was not shifting gears. He tried to get a station on his radio, but either it was too late or the weather, because he couldn't get anything but static.

"Damn," he said and turned it off. "I forget where we are."

"I'll sing for you," Caren offered, her tone too bright. She tossed her cigarette out and rolled up the window. "Like before you had radio." She smiled, giggled, and began to sing "Let the Sunshine In." Joey joined in and I tried to, but couldn't remember the words. The song died. Joey started singing something about "Smiling Faces" that I didn't know. Caren didn't join and his song died, too. Then Joey began to sing a tune about a "Maggie Mae" and I didn't recognize that one, either. Caren smiled and joined in, but they didn't know all the words. Caren and Joey laughed and stopped singing. We passed the bottle around. Caren began to bounce up and down in her seat and clap her hands.

"I must know about this place," she squealed out loud. "I *must* know."

"Not much to know," Joey said, matter-of-fact. "Just an old time house."

"Ooooh," she eyed him. "Really? Like...like in *Gone With The Wind*?"

Joey and I laughed. Caren gave me a puzzled look. I shook my head and looked out my window.

"And what about this old man?" Caren asked.

"He was old and he croaked," Joey said.

Joey laughed and I couldn't help but laugh, too. Caren frowned and pressed her nose against her window. I watched her touch the glass with her tongue as though to lick an ice cream cone. I felt drunk then and felt I didn't belong here. We were alone on a county highway, in a Japanses car, behind its headlights. I knew from memory that beyond the dark was nothing but ravines, pasture and pine trees; and that it once held a sense of place for the likes of me, Foster and others.

Joey turned the car off the highway and onto a muddy road. He didn't hesitate, downshifted, and we sloshed by still, wet, looming oak and hickory trunks in the probing headlights.

"Oooh," Caren said. "Trees are deep and neat."

I stared at her, and then Joey, drunk and not believing what we were doing--going to see an old house in the middle of nowhere and in the wee hours of a morning, after I had just returned from Vietnam, and after all these years. Jared Snead's. I saw his course beard and old teeth, heard his cackle and the *plinking* of piano keys. The old soldier was buried somewhere out here in the dark. In my mind, Foster was buried with him, someone I thought I knew and had listened to all of my life, with the boys and the veterans; who had told the tales and peddled his manners and victuals on the vague porches of my childhood, who wore old clothes, never said a harsh word to anyone; who said "Ma'am" and "Sir" and acted as emcee each year at the Veterans' Ball, steward to the Escatawpha Hunting Lodge, and who removed his hat and stepped off the front steps and into the yard if a lady came to the door and was alone in her house.

"Let's not do this," I said. "Let's go back."

"Nooo," Caren shrilled. "No." She turned and looked at me with an easy smile.

Joey said nothing. We came out of the trees and into a small clearing under starlight, the dark form of the rundown, nineteenth century print house set against the skyline in a yard of dead leaves and high, thick weeds. Joey whipped the sports car through the weeds and braked before the front steps, the porch and dull, doric columns. He cut the lights and the engine.

"I've got to pee," he announced and laughed.

Joey got the flashlight, I had the bottle. We climbed out of the car in the dark, eerie quiet. I lit a cigarette on my Zippo and looked at the silhouettes of the house and trees, feeling like an intruder. Caren laughed and went toward the house. Joey and I placed the bottle and the flashlight on the car's roof, undid our flies and turned away toward the old oaks. I held my cigarette in my mouth as I relieved myself and my eyes adjusted to the light. I looked over to the house of old, weathered wood and columns. The windows were dark but I could make out Caren standing before the steps.

"You remember this place?" I asked Joey.

"Oh, hell, yeah," Joey said as we zipped up.

He took the bottle off the car, took a swallow, gasped, handed it to me. I removed the cigarette from my mouth and took a swallow. We each took another swallow. Joey took the flashlight. I left the bottle on the top of the car. Joey led the way around to Caren.

"You wanted to see it--here it is," Joey declared against the dark stillness. He took her hand. Their feet thudded up the wooden steps onto the porch and to the door.

"Somebody needs to, like you know, paint it," Caren complained.

Joey laughed. "Paint it, hell," he said. "It's going to rot and some redneck's going to put it to the torch."

Joey tried the door and it gave with a jar. "See? Not even locked. Your typical, small South," he pretended to instruct Caren. "We trust in our neighbors."

He turned on the flashlight and led Caren in. I took a quick, last drag off my cigarette, flicked it out into the damp weeds and followed. We stopped in heavy, dank air of the hallway. Joey's searching light showed bare floorboards, a stairway and sallow, cracked walls.

Caren turned, grabbed me and let out a shriek. My heart went to my throat. I thought of Vin Trough's knife. I didn't have it. Joey whirled around, blinding us with the light.

"What?" he yelled.

"There's something in here," Caren moaned.

"Damn," Joey said. "Don't start that ESP crap."

"Oh," Caren moaned, slower and louder. She let go of me. "I feel something here," she said.

"Cut it out," I said.

"There's nothing in here," Joey said. "Rats, maybe. It's empty." He put his arm around her and kissed her hair. "Come on."

Caren whimpered and leaned on him. "This is depressing," she said.

Her hand groped and found my hand behind her. We followed Joey's flashlight past the stairway and through a doorway into the study. Dusty seashells, all different sizes and colors, lined the walls on makeshift shelves of boards and cinder blocks. There was an old army surplus desk and a chair. Something touched my neck. I snatched it. A cord. I pulled it and the ceiling light came on.

"Let there be light," I said.

Joey swayed. He blinked and grinned at me, his eyes bloodshot. He turned off the flashlight and tried to set it on the desk, but it rolled across the top and fell onto the floor. We looked around. The room was stained, dingy, the wood floor was bare. Joey went ahead of us into the next room and turned on the lights. He disappeared into another room. Caren still held my hand.

"Boo," I said in her ear.

She turned and hugged me. "Now, be sweet," she whined. She hugged tighter. "Be sweet."

I slid my hands into her coat and found her ass.

"Oh," she said, burying her head into my chest, "I think we've met before."

"Me, too," I whispered.

She lifted her face and kissed me, giving me tongue. It was quick and easy, like I remembered Vin Trough.

"What are you getting out of this?" I said when she parted.

Caren giggled.

"Hey," Joe yelled from somewhere. "Come on."

Caren turned and I followed her into the large dining room lined with more dusty seashells on shelves, dusty sea-shells stacked in corners, on the worn dining table, on the fireplace mantel, even along the heavy window sills. The fireplace was black and dead and the windows were bare. In the middle of the bare boarded floor was the Jared Snead's family duchesse covered in a sheet and in the corner was the piano with a worn leather seat beside the stained Pier mirror on a dulled brass stand. The piano was dated, small and dark. Caren walked up to it, lifted the keyboard lid and touched a key. *Plunk*, it sounded.

Caren looked around. "Depressing," she frowned.

"Guess the old man liked the sea, huh?" Joey said, entering from the next room. He stopped in his tracks and stared at us. His flushed face and bloodshot eyes went hard. His lips pressed into a thin line.

"Hey," he said, "you like my girl's lipstick on your mouth?"

I touched my mouth. Joey snatched a large seashell from the window and hurled it at me. I ducked it. He glared, threw another one. It went wild.

"Hey," I said.

"Hey, yourself," Joey said, and he rushed me, swinging a haymaker. I stepped aside and he flew past me into the wall and shelves. Joey, shelves and seashells cascaded onto the floor.

Caren screamed. Joey struggled to his feet and whirled around, panting. His bloodshot eyes glared at me and he clenched his fists.

"Hey, don't try it," I said.

"Fuck you."

He charged with another haymaker. Something clicked in me, some anger. I caught him on the wrist, spun under his arm and locked his arm lengthwise behind him, with a swift kick to the stomach and a chop on the back of his neck. He dropped to the floor. Caren screamed. Joey moaned, sighed and slowly staggered up, rubbing his arm and turning to glare at me, his trench coat collar turned up and his hair and headband in disarray.

"Fuck you, man," he uttered, as if that would do something. We stared at each other. Caren stood off watching us with wide eyes and an opened mouth.

"Aw, fuck it," Joey muttered. He spat at me and missed. "Just fuck it and fuck you."

I watched him turn away. "Joey," I said, beginning to feel ashamed.

Joey forced a hard laugh and went into the next room.

"Joey," I yelled after him. My head pounded. My tongue felt thick.

Caren came up beside me. "Well, well," she said. "I would have been one of you, man," she mimicked Joey. She made a mean smile, shot me a parting glance and followed Joey.

I fought an urge to hurt her, too, but I gritted my teeth, took a deep breath and turned away in some memory, some imitation of conduct, walking out of the dingy dining room and through the old study, down the hallway and out onto the old porch, into the still and pale night, the overgrown yard, the dark and old trees with the pale Japanese car and the bottle of Brandy and Benedictine standing on its roof. I stood there on the porch, taking deep breaths, regaining control of myself. By one of the columns, I lit a cigarette on my Zippo and stared out at the night yard, trying to recall this place as it was; and then, on a double-take, I saw Foster's form in something like a blue glow, walking slowly across the yard, among the old oaks in the pale night light. He was in jeans and a tee shirt and his pre-Nam, blonde hair. I stood there while he stopped, turned and grinned at me. I stared at him and he turned and faded into the darkness of the trees. *That's where he went*, I thought. *Going after the likes of Jared Snead.*

I stared at the spot where he disappeared. *Or did he?* I thought.

After a moment, I remembered to smoke my cigarette and I recalled the last time Foster and I were together here before our boot camps and Vietnam. We had hunted squirrels in the overgrown orchard rows beyond this yard on a Saturday morning, in new Ted Williams hunting coats and .410

shotguns. Jared Snead, "The Teller of The Tales," came out of the woods towards us, carrying a glass jug of water in each hand up from the spring, as poor blacks would do, dressed in his shaggy suit coat with his war medals on its lapel, in faded overalls and his limp and battered fedora. He stopped and stared at us with a frown, relaxing his expression and smiling with the old teeth through that coarse beard, setting the jugs down in the dead grass as he recognized us and whose sons we were. He said "Good morning" and we offered him some of the squirrels in our hunting coat packs, but he shook his head no and began to talk. He became expansive and declarative and began to tell us how he loved the mornings, the quiet, the way limbs swung and swayed in the wind in fall light and the way the leaves quivered, as only they could do in the woods; and how he loved to be quiet and listen to the *conk-er-EEs* of blackbirds or the chatter of finches among the tree limbs. He pointed out a large, old oak to us beyond the dirt road that ran behind us, among the other oaks. "That tree," he said, "was here when the Indians were here, when Andrew Jackson camped just over there," he pointed away, "and when Bedford Forrest rode through here, going towards Mississippi."

Foster and I nodded. We had heard it before. We knew our manners, too. "Yes, sir," we said. We smiled and nodded. "Yes, sir."

Jared Snead bent and picked up his jugs. We offered to carry the jugs for him while the three of us walked to the gate and the dirt road. But Jared Snead shook his head and beard no. "I carry my own water," he said. At the gate, we offered him a ride to his house and he shook his head no and then stared at Foster's blue Shelby Cobra Mustang parked in the side rut of the road, outside the rusting wire fence. Jared Snead shook his head in wonder. "Lordy," he drawled, "That thing hurts my eyes."

We made polite laughs. "Yes, sir," we said.

Later, after we unloaded and locked our guns in the trunk, Foster and I laughed in his car, mimicking the speech of Jared Snead--*arrright* for "all right;"words like *yonder, oblige*, or *I give you lief.*

"Give me lief," Foster said.

"And an old oak tree," I said.

We laughed to ourselves and Foster started the blue Shelby Cobra. Its headers boomed to life and droned. We grinned at each other in our new Ted Williams hunting coats and our Dingo boots, taking turns looking into the rearview mirror to comb our hair in what we thought to be the style of Burt Reynolds--our longer hair, our sideburns--before Foster drove the car away from Jared Snead's, going quickly through the gears, spurring up dust behind us on the old dirt road, through the old trees, onto smooth asphalt and checkered lines, and with Booker T and the MGs blaring over the radio.

I woke up in my bed, my eyes and head pounding. I rose and found my way into the bathroom, stuck my finger down my throat and threw up into the toilet. I took some aspirin from the vanity cabinet, gulped water from the faucet, washed my face and made my way out to the kitchen in my sweats, going through the empty and silent house. A note on the refrigerator door told me Mom had gone into town. *Love, Mom.* I looked at the kitchen clock. It was mid-morning. I ate the breakfast Mom left for me in the oven, then walked around the house sipping a cold cup of coffee, looking out the windows at the gray sunlight, feeling the tightness behind my eyes, the lack of sleep; feeling disoriented and useless. I didn't want to turn on the TV and sit still anymore. I wanted to do something, get out.

I showered, shaved, and got dressed, putting on a pair of Dad's work overalls, a pair of heavy socks and field boots, Dad's work coat and gloves. I went outside, through the tail-wagging pointers, to the vehicle shed and cranked up the old two-ton, flatbed truck with the motorized extension ladder. Backing it out, I drove into the cold, gray day, into the rows of the family's pecan trees with their browning leaves, which had been planted by my grandfather and my great-grandfather generations ago--not driving down to the Co-Op to hire on help first, because I didn't want the sight of teenagers to remind me of Foster and myself, and because I wanted to be alone, wanted to feel my own penance with physical work and with my headache for the night before, recalling, as I drove, how Joey and Caren eventually came onto Jared Snead's old porch after I did, screaming, grappling and shouting obscenities at one another about the cot, the night pot and the old photographs they had found lined-up in the kitchen beside a Bible and a bag of salt. Caren broke away from Joey's grasp, ran off the porch and down the steps, where she turned and cried up at both of us from the overgrown, night yard that she wanted to go back into the old house with the lights off, hold hands and have a séance for Jared Snead's spirit in the old kitchen—"to *know*," she wailed, as though it was significant, "where he is." She glared up at me and Joey. She pointed at the house.

Her strange crying animated us. I lit a cigarette and stared at her, smoking too fast, while Joey yelled at her to shut up and that she wasn't going to do shit. He went off the porch and grabbed her by the wrists. I watched while they struggled. Caren screamed "*No.*" "Be nice!" she cried. "Be nice!" She gave me a quick look that reminded me somewhat of Vin Trough's desperate face. I thought of clamping VC's mouths from behind and slitting their throats. I looked at her, grinned and shrugged. Joey caught my look and he grinned, too. He released one of her wrists and slapped her in the face a few times until she submitted with a whimper and climbed into the back of his Japanese car.

"But I *feel* this dead," she cried. "I *feel* this dead."

"Bitch," Joey said. "Bitch." In his anger, he snatched the bottle of Brandy and Benedictine off the roof of the car and he heaved it deep into the night. "We know more about that than you do," he said.

No one spoke as we rode back in a drunken stupor in the Japanese car, while Joey drove through the trees and on the rutted dirt road and onto the highway in the pre-dawn light. Caren sobbed now and then in the back seat while Joey and I sat in the front. No one spoke, even when he let me out at the Oldsmobile in his parents' drive, the dawn light growing stronger. I thought to speak, to turn and wave or do something, but I didn't. Instead, I got into my parents' car, drove home and snuck into my own house, shushing the pointers in the yard to quiet them, and climbing in through my bedroom window like a thief.

Driving the two-ton truck over the dark, desiccated leaves and husks that blanketed the ground, under the cold and gray sky, I parked the idling truck at each spaced-out pecan tree, remembering how to step into the aluminum safety hoop of the flatbed ladder, how to pivot, raise and lower the ladder by the wheel and electronic panel switches. I remembered how to prime and start the power saw, sling its safety strap over my shoulder and cut smaller dead limbs back to an intersecting branch at an angle, the larger dead limbs back to a crown on the trunk. I remembered, too, in the solitude of the trees, how Foster and I used to sometimes be out here, how Marica and I used to be out here, too. I remembered the old town saying that spring never comes to Fermata Bend until pecan trees show their leaves.

Each time I finished a pecan tree; I turned off the power saw, lowered the ladder, stepped off onto the flatbed and set the power saw down. I swung down off the flatbed and picked up the fallen limbs, dragging and hoisting them up onto the flatbed before driving on to the next tree. The work kept me busy, consumed; the coughing and high whine of the power saw while I cut limbs kept me from thinking too much.

I finished the first row of the orchard and began on the second. It began to grow colder while I worked down the row. After some time, I braked the truck across from the small and rusted iron fence my great-grandfather put up to set the slave graveyard of simple and crude stones apart from the pecan trees. In the aluminum hoop, I cut off three limbs on a tree. I turned off the power saw, lowered the ladder by the panel switch and stepped off onto the flatbed. It was in this place, I remembered Jared Snead's tale, in a forest, before a long gone house, that General Beauregard's army camped toward the end of the Civil War and he was invited by Jared Snead's forebears to a corn and catfish dinner at Jared Snead's home place. The general danced with the ladies and played "Lorena"and "The Yellow Rose of Texas" for the family on the piano, songs that Jared Snead's mother and then Jared Snead continued to play. Men died of their wounds on the town square and in the churches set up as hospitals. They were buried in the town cemetery. The town and the soldiers got ready for a battle which never happened and when the general had to retreat further west, he gave a sword to the community with a speech, thanking them for their hospitality. He called Fermata Bend "A soldier's town". Since then, Fermata Bend families--most of all, the men--had told that tale, as well as others. Fermata Bend inspired its sons on history and heroes.

Fermata Bend Family women swore allegiance to and waited for their men when they left to fight. And Fermata Bend, I thought to myself, had been turning boys into brave soldiers ever since.

I tried to imagine what it was like way back then. I imagined Jared Snead playing the family piano as a young boy before I saw him playing it as an old man for us boys and our fathers after the deer drives. Then something of Marica came to me: her grinning and singing "My Green Tambourine," and her red braids flying behind her on horseback. I held her hand as we walked in the pasture. I remembered how Foster and I stopped for lunch before my great-grandfather's cast iron fence on a warmer day while we were spreading fertilizer over the grounds from the spreader truck. Three or four years ago. We sat in our dusty overalls and work boots against the corroded iron bars and we had ham sandwiches and cokes. We joked and laughed. We threw wadded Tootsie Roll papers at one another while "Sunshine of Your Love" and "The Letter" played from WLS on the truck's radio.

I heard the car before I saw it. The maroon Oldsmobile seemed to come out of nowhere, glide down the long orchard row toward me, its tires crunching the dark, decayed leaves and husks; the overcast light seeming to coalesce on its dead headlights, its windshield and chrome rims reflecting the passing pecan trees and sky. From the flatbed, I watched the car stop a few yards away. Mom waved behind the windshield and the steering wheel. *Hi*, she mouthed and smiled.

I turned the chainsaw off as she cut the engine and got out of the car, closing the driver's door and coming forward in her long, beige overcoat, with a bright orange scarf around her neck and dark brown pumps from her going into town.

She smiled up at me with her light, red lips; her tired eyes; her steel hair in a new and close perm.

"Mom, what brings you out here?"

"Hey," she said. She stopped before the truck and folded her arms. "Glad I could catch you out here." She paused. "Can I talk to you?" she said. "Can you come down?"

I lifted the strap off my shoulder and set the chain saw down on the flatbed along the freshly cut and stacked pecan limbs. I placed my gloved hands on the edge of the flatbed and swung down to the ground.

"So," she paused. "You've decided to help Dad out?"

I nodded. "I thought I should start."

Mom nodded. She made a smile and hesitated. Then she gave me her hard look, her face suddenly drawn and intent under her new perm. "James Beckwith Senecal," she said slowly," her voice soft and terse. "You are going to shame your father," she stated.

I watched her face and the corner of her lip tremble.

"Mom, I—"

"You know," she interrupted, "that in Fermata Bend men need men to tell them what they are. You've come too far now to pretend otherwise," her voice rose to a trill. "You served your country," she nodded, "and you spent an extra year there for the memory of your best friend." She nodded. "That's honorable," she said. "Now, don't shame you father now in the process, before the whole town." Mom shook her head. "He doesn't deserve that," she said. "No one deserves that."

"Mom, I...."

"You don't have to worry about shaming *me*," she continued, her voice remaining high and shrill. She gave me a dismissive wave with her hand. "We women know who we are," she said, nodding. "You men may think you tell us what we are, too. And what you did the other morning," she added, "I can keep to myself." She nodded faster as she grew teary-eyed. "The only way you can shame me now," she said, "would be in the way you treat another woman--

"But your father," she wouldn't let me talk, "you can shame him easily just because he's a man and you're his son." She stopped nodding and held her eyes on me. "You know it's never ending," she said. "You know, as well as I do, you always have to measure up. Your father wants to be proud of you."

She glared at me. "He has too much to explain if you don't go to the parade," she said simply. "Don't you do this to him." Mom paused. "Not now. Not after all this town has been through the last few years. All those boys. Don't you do this to Foster," she added.

"Mom," I said. "Mom, it isn't like that." I looked into her face.

"It isn't like that?" Her stare turned incredulous. "What do you mean? What is it like?"

"I don't know how to act anymore."

"Act?" she said. She stared. "Act? Lordy, that's what we're asking you to do, *act*. You act like always," she said. "You act like Foster would."

"What was always?" I asked. "How do I do that?"

"Beck," Mom sighed, shaking her head. "Beck, war has always been hard. But you come back. You go on," she said. "Because...because you *have* to."

"Maybe you did back then," I said. "When you could see what you were doing."

"See?" Mom echoed, nonplused. "Why wouldn't you see what you were doing? It's your duty. It's right."

I looked at the tired, staring insistence of her face and eyes and fought back a bitter laugh. I turned away and leaned against the edge of the flatbed, struggling for control, sighing, smiling and shaking my head, seeing the trees with their browning leaves, the sky, my great-grandfather's corroded iron fence and the simple, crude stones, and thinking, for some reason, of people saluting, seeing old men saluting in nondescript uniforms, Jared Snead, my father, Foster, and all the veterans of Fermata Bend; how people always smiled and waved from passing cars on the highway and sang together in church before and since I had come home; how people like Vin Trough, Dea and Abbie could smile, even when they didn't want to; how Jared Snead, Foster, Reverend Hirsch and men and women seemed to all smile, and then how it felt to want a joint or a drink or a cigarette so bad--like now--something with a deep hit to stay or numb a feeling of waste.

While my mother looked on, I fished a cigarette out of the pack in my overall vest pocket and lit it on my Zippo from my pants pocket. I took a deep, fast drag.

"Beck," Mom said behind me. "You're one of us," she said it calmly. "No matter where you go or what you think, you are one of us."

I turned to her, smoking deep and fast, looking at her plaintive face and eyes, and thought of my father's face, the way I used to look up to it as a boy, and I felt how long ago three, four years had become.

I smoked deep and fast and we looked at each other.

"Well," Mom said, after a moment, her tone and her face resigning. She took a deep breath, bowed her head and closed her eyes, as though in resolve, folding her arms tighter against her coat. "All right. I'm going to ask you," she said, keeping her eyes closed, pacing her words, slow, tense and deliberate. "Walk in the parade with your father," she said. "Please."

She opened her eyes, her look apprehensive, fearful.

We looked at one another. I sighed. I could not refuse that far. "All right, Mom," I said. "All right."

Mom smiled with slow relief. She nodded and wiped her eyes. "Everything will be all right again, Beck," she assured me. "You'll see," she promised. She hesitated, put out her arms, came forward and hugged me. "Everything will be all right," she said in my ear.

She stepped back, smiling, and then, didn't seem to know what else to say.

I nodded. "Okay," I said.

"Okay," she said. She nodded, too. "I'll have your lunch," she reminded me smiling. She turned away and I watched her go, walking slowly to the car. Before the driver's door, she stopped and looked toward her grandfather's cast iron fence.

"Do you know the story?" she asked. "There was a house here."

"General Beauregard," I said. "He camped."

Mom looked back at me. "Yes." She shrugged. "Oh, well. You men know about that."

I didn't say anything, but watched as she got into the car and drove away, through soft and decaying leaves.

Veterans' Day afternoon was sunny and cool. In my khaki Ranger cap and uniform, which Mom had pressed again for me that morning, and wearing my Ray Bans and my polished boots, I kept step beside her in the column of wives and mothers of Fermata Bend Veterans while we marched in a slow four-step to Dad's spaced, heavy beats on Jared Snead's old bass drum, ahead of us in the parade. I held my eyes ahead, my back rigid and my shoulders squared, feeling isolated and self-conscious, as though everyone's eyes were on me, as I used to feel in church, growing up here, at school assembly or during high school ball games. Now and then, I would look ahead and see Dad leading the front column of Fermata Bend Veterans: middle-aged white men in their ankle boots, business suits and blue veterans' caps; their faces solemn and forward, diligently stepping in unison behind the town's yellow fire truck and the leading, flashing blue lights of the slow-rolling police car.

Dad had smiled and saluted me that morning as I came into the kitchen in my uniform. Then without a word and with a still face, he gave me my grandfather's Pershing Army watch. I looked at him and nodded. "Thank you, Dad," I said and strapped it on my wrist.

"There you are, soldier," he beamed. "I'm going to tell the boys to let you lead the parade. You're coming in late," he admitted with a big smile. "But they'll let you."

I smiled and shook my head no. "You go on ahead," I said. "Like you said, I'm coming in late. I'd just mess things up. I'll walk with mom."

Dad's smile fell a little. "Walk with Mom?" He paused. "You sure? Well--okay," he shrugged, sighed. "If that's what you want. Make your mother proud," he winked. "But don't worry, we'll have you up front with us next year."

I had smiled and nodded, too.

Mom clutched my arm now and again while we walked, bearing a constant smile of red lipstick to the various on-lookers on the sidewalks, in an auburn princess dress with a matching belt and wearing a ginger-colored, cartwheel hat. Instead of high heels, she wore soft leather shoes. All the wives and mothers with us in the parade were like that, smiling in nice, new dresses and soft shoes; hats and lipstick, waving red, white and blue streamers in their hands as the parade went down Main Street and around the town square, circling the old war memorial obelisk with its engraved names; the faded, flapping flags on their poles, the World War I artillery piece and the stained Confederate statue. Townspeople, in their plain or business clothes, smiled and waved from the sidewalks, standing behind the parking meters spiraled in red, white and blue ribbons and before printed banners and soaped Veterans' Day slogans on the shop windows, like LEST WE FORGET, FREEDOM FOREVER and A SOLDIER'S TOWN .

Before the parade, in the old armory yard, where we gathered to line up, women had kissed and exclaimed and hugged me, and men had gripped my hand. "Beck! Welcome back!" they had all said. "Welcome back!" "We've wondered where you got off to!" "We're proud of you, boy!" Some women came out of nowhere, like Miss Bolton, Foster's and my third grade teacher, and hugged me hard without a word and cried. Our short, thin, and aging mayor, Mr. Casey, in his suit and veteran's cap, had cut through the crowd to exclaim my name, grin and clutch my elbow. Mr. Alberton, the rural mailman, had kept his big smile while shaking my hand again and again. Reverend Hirsch had come forward, too, and welcomed me back home. "We've missed you," he said. He took both my hands in his and bowed his head in a quick prayer others could hear. "Oh, Lord, we thank you," he said. "Beck Senecal has come home to Fermata Bend. Lord, we celebrate and we pray, and we do it especially for those who will not be coming back."

"Yes," I said and nodded. *We,* I thought.

As we walked in the parade, I knew from the armory yard that behind the wives and mothers of the parade came the line of convertibles: a sky blue Corvette, a yellow Thunderbird, a silver Cadillac El Dorado, and a red Volkswagen Beetle, each one with a waving beauty queen in a new fall suit and driven by a veteran, and each car with advertising posters on the doors, such as for the local radio station, the VFW post, and the Fermata Bend Co-Op. Behind the convertibles came smiling cheerleaders marching in tight blue sweaters, skirts and tennis shoes, holding a long banner between them that stretched the width of the road, reading in blue on white: FERMATA BEND: A SOLDIER'S TOWN. And I knew from the armory yard that after the cheerleaders came the

majorettes with batons, in glittering, silver suits and blue-tas-
seled, white ankle boots; the flag-bearing Honor Guard of
boys in gray cadet uniforms, stern faces and silver helmets
with thick, white chin straps; and then the high school band
in their blue and white uniforms with matching hats and
plumes, stepping in sharp, strident steps and in columns of
four. They kept striking up "Over There" or "The Stars and
Stripes Forever," their music sheets clipped onto their instru-
ments.

Behind the band, came the flatbed truck floats of cos-
tumed high school students in Fermata Bend war moments
of history: Andrew Jackson pointing a sword at Indians, the
Nineteenth Century townspeople of Fermata Bend prepar-
ing breastworks under the eye of General Beauregard for the
battle that never happened, Dough Boys in uniforms and pith
helmets, carrying rifles in a dirt, barbed-wired battlefield; and
then a colorful, paper-and-wire version of the flag raising at
Iwo Jima. Finally, the rear of the parade was brought up by
a half-dozen of Mrs. Julie Brown's young Equestrian School
students, decked out as Rough Riders on their horses, a final
police car, and then a donkey-driven cart full of Fermata Bend
High football players in their home jerseys, grinning and toss-
ing out free American Flag patches.

As Dad led the way on a second lap around the square,
I relaxed and chanced glances to faces on the sidewalks, but
I didn't find Marica. I saw familiar, older, smiling faces in
dated clothes. I saw Abbie Stewart standing with others at
Brown's Drug Store in something like a green suit and her
blonde hair. She gave me a long, impervious stare and turned
away. I recognized Randall Lowe, in dark hair, dark slacks
and a light dress shirt, who had served in Vietnam two years
before my class and now helped run his father's hardware

store. He nodded and gave me a shadow of a salute. I nodded back. Why wasn't he in the parade? I recognized a petite, brunette girl I had gone to high school with, in jeans and a jacket, and holding a bundled infant on her hip. She nodded to me and gave me a peace sign. A mutt dog barked at us from the meridian of the square. Children I did not recognize played at the curb.

In front of Minnie's Clothing Store, I saw Dale Kevin in a crowd of farmers, looking rough with an unshaven face; long, honey hair and his hands stuck into the trouser pockets of his green maintenance clothes. He shook his head as though he knew something I didn't. He had served in Vietnam a year ahead of me. And why wasn't he in the parade? I wondered. Then I saw Dea, standing in front of a telephone pole, all by herself, with her big, loud and blonde Afro; grinning from ear-to-ear with her gapped teeth like a Cheshire cat, in something like a fluorescent yellow gown with orange bar-patterns and heavy, metal bracelets. She waved to me with both hands, jangling her bracelets. Mother smiled and waved back. I nodded.

With my mom's arm in mine, we slowly circled the town square with the parade again. I looked out to the people on the sidewalks through my Ray Bans, but I didn't see Marica. Some days ago, I had bought a new car battery at Mort's Texaco filling station and a car tag at Town Hall, smiling and enduring old Mort Wilson's loud greetings, his garrulous voice and grin as he asked me questions, wiped my windshield and checked my oil; and then the Town Hall secretary's recognition and praise, too. Since then, I had been driving up and down the county highway late at nights, alone and smoking in my old Camaro; and each night, driving by Marica's house, too--two, three, sometimes more times--letting the engine drone in neutral as I coasted by, looking to the front door, to the cars there: her parents' green LTD, her yellow Barracuda; wondering if the blue Plymouth GTX in the drive was that other guy's, Roddy Whats-His-Name, or maybe her younger brother's. Each time I drove by, nothing changed. I looked at the quiet and once-familiar yard and watched for the lights in the windows, letting the car coast as slow as I dared, until there was nothing else to do but downshift and drive on.

"Do you see Lisa Nanner?" My mother looked up at me with a whisper, still holding her smile.

I shook my head no.

"Oh, I thought she might come," Mom paused with a pensive look. "Maybe," she considered, "maybe it's too much."

I nodded and realized if Foster were here, as he once was--and Curtis and Johnny and Bubba--I might be into it, too. Was in it, at one time. Believed in it. I remembered the night, my junior year, when I thought the entire town crowded onto the square and stopped our team bus after we upset Citronelle, 9-6. Foster, Bubba, and I led the football players off the bus and the team circled the square in our blue sweat tops, jeans and tennis shoes. The street lights were on and our elation teemed in the cool, night air, and it seemed as though everyone I had ever known cheered and waved to us from the sidewalks. On the median, the high school band in plain clothes played "Stars Fell on Alabama" and then "Hang 'em High." Marica broke from the crowd in front of Brown's Drug Store and came running at no one but me--my red-headed girl with a huge smile. She hugged my neck. Foster and I grinned, waved and slapped each other on the back. Abbie joined us, too, and we lapped the square together. We were worthy, we were loved. Everyone smiled.

"Hold your head up, smile," Mom said through her own smile. "People are watching you."

As the parade rounded the square and wound back up onto Main Street, we passed four black men watching the parade around the corner fire hydrant at the bank, in their faded overalls, boots and field shirts. I had bailed hay with one of them, but he didn't seem to see me. I thought, likely, more than one of them had served, too; but this was mostly a white man's thing, after all.

We slowly marched past the bank and followed the parade up Main Street, past the Co-Op, Joneses' Cleaners, the old frame houses and into the armory yard where the parade had begun. The band stopped playing and the floats began pulling off to the side of the street. The parade began to break up, people began to mill and scatter. Only, ahead of everyone, my father and the veterans didn't stop marching, didn't look back. They continued stepping behind the fire truck and the slow and flashing lights of the police car, without pause and in procession toward the highway and Jared Snead's home place to hold the vigil.

"Hold your head up, smile," Mom said. She still smiled as we stood in the armory yard. Someone waved to us across the street. Mom waved and then I waved back. After a moment, Mom and I made our way to our Oldsmobile in the Joneses' Cleaners parking lot. We stopped, smiled and spoke to the Shoffs, an elderly couple. "Welcome home, Beck!" they clamored. I thanked them. "We're proud of you." Then I thought I heard someone call my name. I turned, but could not recognize a face in the dispersing crowd of teenagers; could not even be sure that it had been meant for me.

In my hot rod Camaro, still in uniform, cap and sunglasses from the parade, I drove out to Jared Snead's place
to deliver the coffee and sandwiches Mom had prepared for
the veterans' vigil. I had driven Mom home in our Oldsmobile from the parade, waiting behind the other cars and stop
lights, slowing the car outside of town on the county highway
and waiting in line to pass the slow marching procession of
the veterans in step behind the fire truck and the police car.
Mom and I caught a glimpse of Dad as we drove by, his face
still resolved, his eyes focused ahead with a purpose while he
beat time on Jared Snead's old drum.

"There's your dad," Mom had drawled, slow and matter-of-fact. She had sighed, too, her cartwheel hat beside her
on the front seat. She had touched her center hairpiece and
glanced back at him as we drove away.

Turning off the highway onto the back roads in the
Camaro, I went through the gears, feeling the revving of the
engine and the droning of the headers, turning onto the still
muddy drive through the old oaks toward the home place.
In the overgrown clearing, Jared Snead's house sat like a dull,

vacant shell of peeling paint with columns. The high, dead grass and weeds of the lawn had been pressed down and rutted from vehicles turning around in it. A navy blue GMC pickup truck with a white camper unit on its bed was parked in the muddy drive along the cedar trees that lined the rusted wire fence of the winter pasture and the Snead family plot.

I parked the Camaro behind the camper pickup, noting a dozen or so men in overcoats now, ankle boots and blue veteran caps, standing and talking beyond the cedars, in the overgrown pasture and the dull gravestones, two acting as sentries with shouldered Springfields by the newer tombstone with a mound of faded, piled wreaths. A few feet off each corner of that grave, and behind the guards, was a smoking, oil-burning wick canister on top of a pole. A white tent had been pitched beyond the grave plot into the wet trees. A lamp burning within it made a pale glow through the cloth. The scene looked eerie and antedated. I cut the engine, set the parking brake and got out of the car with the cardboard box of two large coffee thermos, paper cups, napkins and wrapped sandwiches.

"Hey," Dad called to me. He parted from a group of veterans and came forward to meet me at the line of the old wire fence in the cedar trees.

In his heavy overcoat and veterans cap, my Dad grinned. "Whew," he said, sighing and shaking his head with relief, like someone taking a break from hard work. "We need that now," he declared softly. He nodded to me, took one of the paper cups and tilted coffee into it from one of the thermoses while I held the box. He took quick, grateful sips from the cup, looked back to the others, then at me.

"It's going to be a haul," he said, chatty and energetic. "Supposed to freeze tonight. But we'll make it," he winked. "In shifts."

I smiled and nodded. I looked to see the other men. Everything had the feel of a bivouac. My father drained the cup, set it in the box and took the box from me.

"You want to come join us?" he asked with a nod.

I shook my head no. "No thanks. I'll sit this one out."

"Okay," Dad grinned. "Okay, you take a rest. You've earned it," he said. "I'm proud of you," he winked. "We'll get you later. We'll get you into the Fermata Bend post and then in our Guard unit." He winked. "After a little rest," he added and smiled. "After a little rest."

I grinned for him and watched him turn with the box to the other veterans around the grave plot and the tent, watched the men gather around him, taking sandwiches and pouring coffee into paper cups. I watched them begin to talk and joke. One of them waved to me.

I turned away, fished a cigarette out of my uniform shirt pocket, lit it on my Zippo and walked slowly up the washed-out chert drive along the overgrown lawn and the oaks to the front steps, the dull wood and chipped paint of Jared Snead's house, remembering, for some odd reason, humming the Beatles' "I'll Follow the Sun," on a lazy summer day here when Foster and Edmond and I rode Jared Snead's Tennessee Walkers bareback about this yard as kids; then the camp stew, hunting boots, tobacco smoke, the laughter of men in wool plaid hunting shirts in the crisp, fall air after a hunt; men and boys talking and exclaiming, bragging and laughing about the yard, house and porch. I heard the *plinking* of Jared Snead's piano keys. I heard his long and low whistle, as though to sound an exclamation.

I walked around the side of the house, through the high, dead grass. The wire dog pens were vacant. Some of the house's window panes were broken, the long sideboards were gray and peeling. Beer cans and bottles were scattered about the ground and there were cold ashes from a fire. I noticed someone had spray painted "Suze lost it here 10-9-70" and "We Are Great!" in red with their gnarled initials on the slave-made chimney brick. Joe McDowell had been right, I thought. It would rot and burn.

I circled the house back to the front, smoking and looking for the pegs in the wood as I remembered them. At the steps to the clapboard porch with the weathered columns, I sat down and flicked my cigarette butt into the stillness of the weed-choked drive. It was too still and quiet. I took off my Ranger's cap and threaded it into the shoulder lapel of my coat, took off my RayBans, folded them and put them into my coat pocket, trying to imagine what the place once was, and trying to imagine if three years ago I would have believed I would be here like this now. Beyond the overgrown lawn and oaks trees, the small flames, slow-moving figures and soft glow from the tent within the cedars around the cemetery plot appeared hazy, ghoulish. I looked on the scene in the dying light and my mind invaded with the growing, *wop-wop-wopping* sounds of Hueys; the waiting and palled faces of my platoon buddies in their fatigues and helmets.

Dea came slowly out of the trees in her two-door, white Lincoln, smiling with her gapped teeth and the convertible top down. She stopped her car behind my Camaro and the camper pickup at the line of cedars. I could make out *Pecan Tree Real Estate 288-1103* in purple on the Lincoln's door. I watched her get out of the car with two large paper sacks in her arms, in flared blue jeans with a matching denim jacket, a white belt, and a white blouse. Her loud, blonde Afro. She left her driver's door opened, stopped with a sack in each arm, still smiling, and she peered about and up toward me at the house. Something gold was on her neck. I watched as she turned and went into the cedars, to the grave plot and the veterans. I unbuttoned my coat, fished a cigarette from my shirt pocket and lit it on my Zippo. In a few moments, Dea came out empty-handed and still smiling. She stood with her hands on her hips and gazed toward me. I sat and smoked while she got back into the Lincoln, shut the door, and turned the car into the overgrown drive. The Lincoln came toward the house and pulled up beside me. Dea braked hard and stared across at me from the steering wheel.

"Hi, soldier." She made a small smile and a wave.

"Hi, yourself. What brings you out here?"

"What do you mean...what brings me out here?" she said. "I brought refreshments for the *white* men," she stressed. She paused with a broader smile, her ice blue lips and eyelids. She had something like a gold collar on her neck. "I'm going to sell this place, baby," Dea said, matter-of-fact. "Lisa Nanner doesn't want it no more."

"Who does?" I said. "It's overgrown, too far gone."

Dea's smile fell. "Don't you believe it," she shook her head in quick disagreement. "It means something to some-body," she said, her voice going shrill. "It'll mean something to me to sell it," she smiled. "I lived down the road from here in a shack all my life," Dea said, nodding, "taking hand-me-downs and my daddy doing odd jobs and we hearing all our lives about this land, this town, this family--

"Now," she smiled and nodded, "I'm the one who's going to sell the very place they were made of... and everything with it. With a little luck, it'll mean something to some stuck up, black person or some rich Yankee or some doctor's wife with nothing better to do but own Jared Snead's place and think they can restore history."

"Restore it?" I shook my head.

"Restore it," Dea nodded.

"Restore it?" I said in disbelief. "It's past the point, Dea."

"*Restore* it," Dea insisted. She nodded with a smug look. "You wait. You wait and see."

I looked at her smile of gapped teeth, sighed and looked at the trees and the overgrown yard.

"Well, good luck, Dea," I said, turning to her. I took a long draw off my cigarette.

Dea held a hard smile and nodded fast. "You just wait," she said. "You just wait and see."

She gave me a wink and a smile, sure of herself. She put both hands on the wheel and drove away. I watched the Lincoln cut a swath through the dead weeds on the old drive, the back of Dea's blonde Afro standing out like a sponge behind the wheel of that big, white car with its painted signs on the doors. She drove fast, past the camper truck and my Camaro, and disappeared into the old trees toward the highway.

I shook my head in disbelief, stubbed my cigarette out on the wooden porch step and flicked it into the dead weeds. Gazing out at the yard, the shadowy figures and the flickering lights beyond the line of cedars, I thought there was nothing else to do but get up and go home.

A yellow Barracuda with a hard roof came out of the trees. It slowed and seemed to barely roll down the muddy drive. It turned in behind my Camaro and parked. I looked on, thinking to take another cigarette out of my shirt pocket while a young woman with red hair got out of the driver's side of the car and shut the door. She looked over the top of the car in my direction and I forgot my cigarette. Her hair was smooth and shorter now, in bangs. She carried a large paper bag in both arms, and she was in dark brown knee boots, a deep green crew sweater and a champagne colored skirt with a wide, brown belt.

I stared at where she disappeared into the line of trees and didn't move. When she re-emerged from the cedars, empty-handed, I stood up and watched her stop, look to my Camaro, up toward me and turn to her car. I thought to shout, to run, but all I could do was stand rooted on the step as she got into the Barracuda, shut the driver's door and started the engine. The car backed up and braked. It turned into Dea's plowed wake on the overgrown drive. I stood on the porch step as she drove the car up and braked in front of me. Marica cut the engine and got out slowly, leaving the driver's door opened, and she stepped up on the running board.

"Hi," she said quietly, over the top of the car.

I stared, nodded. Her small smile, her hair. Her gray eyes. She wore darker eyelashes and she had on something like beige lipstick.

"You want I should leave?" she said after a moment.

I shook my head no.

"Well," Marica said. She stepped back and off from the running board, closed the driver's door and came around the rear of the car toward me. She went up past me on the steps and onto the porch, stopped and turned to me at the first peeling column with a small, wry grin.

"I hear you driving by at night," she said. She smiled. "There's only one car that sounds like that."

I nodded.

She shrugged. "So, why don't you stop? Or come to the door?" She watched me with her steady gray eyes.

"You're engaged," I managed.

"Ha." Marica laughed and shook her head. "Ha. No," she informed me. "I'm not engaged. At least, not anymore."

Her smile went small and thin. "I got engaged for the wrong reasons," she said and paused. "I couldn't go through with it," she admitted.

"But look at you," she changed the topic, her tone going friendly and bright. "All different and in uniform." She smiled and nodded. "And here I am...doing all the talking," she said. "Why are you so quiet?"

I could only look at her and shake my head.

She made that small, wry smile of hers, looked away into the overgrown yard and then back at me.

"I know you loved him," she said quietly. "Or yourself," she paused, nodding, "or it...or whatever it was. I know you loved it and you loved your home town." She nodded, sighed, pressed her lips into a thin line. "You had to live with yourself," she nodded. "I know.

"Fermata Bend does that to people," she said with a nod. "Everyone belongs and everyone knows..." Marica kept nodding. "Like I know..." she shrugged. "Like I know how much you loved Saturday nights, The Beatles...*The Man From Uncle* and Dell comic books." She paused and smiled at me. "You loved The Association, The Moody Blues and Marvin Gaye."

She watched me. "You loved fast cars, hunting and football. And Dion."

Dion? I tried to remember.

"You loved going down by the river," she rambled on, "chicken and dumplings," she said. "*Cool Hand Luke, The Fantastic Voyage* and *The Longest Day.*" She looked away into the yard. "You loved to sit and talk in your car," she said. "You loved to sit on my parents' porch...."

"I loved you," I said.

She shook her head. "Don't lie."

"I'm not trying to lie."

She seemed not to hear me. She made a sad smile. "So, are you here to stay?" she asked.

I shook my head no.

Marica nodded. "Me, neither," she informed me. "One time, I thought I might get a degree from the junior college, then a husband, a house and a baby." She made a nervous laugh. "But now, I'm going to Birmingham to become a pharmacist. First girl in the family to follow her father's footsteps," she added. "First girl."

"Oh?" I nodded. "Are you? Well, good," I managed. "That's good for you."

We smiled and nodded at one another. Then, for an eerie moment, it seemed as though we had been standing there forever, rock still and looking at one another, never breathing or speaking. I saw Marica's lips part, begin to move to form a word, and I did not want that moment to go. I stepped forward and pressed her hard against me, feeling the rustle of her blouse under the sweater and her body against mine, closing my eyes against her neck and the brush of her hair, smelling her moist skin of Dove soap, the same scent of Wind Song perfume. I had come a long way to smell her again. I wanted to hear her sing "My Green Tambourine".

"Beck," I heard her from far off. "Beck."

I parted. Marica was crying and trying to smile.

"Can I carry you?" I asked.

"Carry me?" she said.

I bent and scooped her up in my arms. She let out a surprised squeal and gripped my shoulders with both hands.

"Beck," she warned. "What are you doing?"

I turned to Jared Snead's old door. "I 'm going to carry you over the threshold," I said with a grin.

"Carry me?" she gave me an incredulous look. She

glanced in the direction of the veterans in the winter pasture. She had no choice but to put her arms around my neck.

"Beck," Marica warned.

I grinned and didn't give a damn. I walked to the door and butted it open with my foot, turned her sideways and carried her in, down the dark, musty hallway, through the study cluttered with seashells, and into the living room, its bare floorboards and bare, tall, dirty windows with no drapes, streaming dull light into a floating myriad of dust motes; General Beauregard's piano, the covered duchesse and the stained, brass Pier mirror on its stand.

"*Beck.*"

I laughed, set her down on the dusty, covered duchesse and kissed her. She pushed me away. I kissed her again.

"No, Beck," she shook her head. "No, this is no good," she said, startled, as though realizing something. "It's just memory," she said.

I looked at her face and wondered what else was there? Her memory. My memory. I wondered what happened to Foster's memory when a VC sniper took his mind. I kissed her again and this time she didn't push me away. After a few moments, she put her arms around me and kissed me back. We kissed and held each other in the old, still house.

"Okay," she laughed, after a while, with a soft whisper, a soft gasp. She parted from me. I opened my eyes to her gray eyes, the smeared lipstick of her mouth; her short, mussed hair.

"Okay," she laughed with a nod of her head, her voice relenting. "You call me, okay?" She touched my cheek. "We'll start over again, okay? You can come see me in Birmingham," she nodded. "You write me in Birmingham."

I nodded. There wasn't anything else to do.

"Is there any difference between them and us?" I asked, nodding in the direction of the veterans.

"Oh," Marica shrugged and sighed. "Probably not. They've just stayed here too long."

She smiled and touched her hair. I watched her step away from the duchesse and walk away from me, through the soft window light and floating dust motes to Jared Snead's old, brass Pier Mirror. She stopped and studied herself in the stained mirror, fingering her hair and wiping her lips with her fingers. She cocked her knee at rest like she used to do. She turned and glanced at me with a quick smile.

"Old house," she commented, looking past me and around at the windows.

She turned back to mirror to touch her hair, nod and smile at herself. I nodded, too, in some vague agreement to what I thought was something mutual: our common thoughts, our common memories, our town. Marica's hands dropped; her smooth face slowly swept the room from the mirror. Her face stopped on me, smiled, and I looked at her, knowing then that whatever we knew, whatever we had shared; it would not be the same, it could not go anywhere.

That moment in November of 1971, before Jared Snead's home place would eventually rot, fall in and burn; before my mother and father would grow senile and die, the World War II and Korean veterans of Fermata Bend would all age and die, and names like Bubba Smith would be listed as Missing In Action forever on a stone or a piece of paper somewhere—I felt the heavy and final weight of The Disconnect, a feeling that sunk deep into the pit of me thereafter, telling me I would never belong to a community again.

People like Vin Trough would go the way of the millions who perished unaccounted for in Southeast Asia. Cars and

songs and TV shows would come and go. I would lose contact with the likes of Joe McDowell, Edmond Banes and Abbie Stewart, and Foster Odom would become something like
a vision of a boy, existing in the back of my mind as a time
forever small town, rural and impressionable: a lone, grinning
boy in blue, turning away into some semblance of old woods,
after some semblance of legend, like those of Desoto, Andrew
Jackson and Bedford Forrest. Dea would never marry and
one day become the first black and female mayor of Fermata
Bend, Alabama. Small industries moved in. Outsiders moved
in. The new Interstate would come through Jared Snead's old
land, bringing with it things like housing projects, an outlet
mall, a self-serve filling station, a Hardee's and a Walmart.

I remember the moment I watched Marica touch the ends
her short, red bangs and turn away from the mirror with a
quick, bemused smile, her gray eyes a passing glance. Over
the decades, we have seen each other when we come back to
Fermata Bend from other cities to weddings, class reunions
and funerals, each time with calmer and aged faces, different
interests and different hair, with or without spouses, with or
without something to talk about; a brief hug, a polite question or two, as though to seek a vague comfort from one
another, as though to confirm from one another whatever is
left of ourselves and memory.

"I think of you, Beck," Marica will whisper to me, each
time with a slight pause, a soft wane of a smile. "You were the
boy," she will say. "You were the boy who chose Foster over
me."

Each time, I smile and nod to be polite. And I will
wonder. I will recall times, places and faces--but looking
back on it, I do not recall choosing anything at all. I recall
being young and like someone else and acting on feelings

and impulses that now seem irrelevant. Sometimes I will see something like a Jared Snead in my mind, too. He is standing before an old tree or in an overgrown field, an old, dated man in a shaggy suit coat with war medals, wearing a battered fedora; his dark eyes on me, his rough beard and mouth moving, but uttering no sound.

A native of Jacksonville, Alabama, Theron Montgomery is the author of *The Procession* and *Driving Truman Capote*. He has been the Founding Editor of the *Alabama Literary Review*, Chief Editor of the *Alabama English Journal* and Fiction Editor of the *Blue Moon Review*. He is a professor of Contemporary Literature and creative writing at Troy University.